"You've Seen Me In A Swimsuit. It's Not A Big Deal."

He couldn't stop his eyes from roaming over her bare skin and that valley between her breasts. When he met her gaze again, he didn't see desire like he'd hoped—he saw uncertainty.

"You must've really hit your head," she joked, but the smile failed to meet the expectation of the joke. "You've never talked like this before or looked at me like...like..."

"Like what?" he murmured.

"Like you want me."

"I know exactly what I'm saying and what I want, Piper." He purposely let his eyes drop to her mouth as he slid his hand up and over her bare shoulder. "You know how special you are in my life and how much I value our friendship."

"Then why are you looking at me like you want to kiss me?" she whispered.

* * *

To Tame a Cowboy is a
Texas Cattleman's Club: The Missing Mogul novel.

Love and scandal meet in Royal, Texas!

* * *

If you're on Twitter,
tell us what you think of Harlequin Desire!
#harlequindesire

Dear Reader,

My response when I was asked to be part of the amazing Texas Cattleman's Club continuity series? Yes, please! Writing about hunky, sometimes rebellious Texans and the women who want to tame them... How could I say no?

You may already be familiar with Ryan, the hot rodeo star, and Piper, the hometown paramedic. These two have been best of friends since Piper socked Ryan in the eye in grade school. But you know what they say about best friends...they make the best lovers. :-)

Getting to know these two characters with their push-pull relationship was such a pleasure. With Ryan's laid-back cowboy attitude and Piper's feistiness, I couldn't wait for them to realize they were a match made in polar-opposite heaven.

This series was such a joy to work on with so many talented authors and friends. I do hope you enjoy Ryan and Piper's friends-to-lovers story as much as I loved writing it.

For more information on any of my books, check out my website, www.julesbennett.com. I love hearing from readers, so drop me a line!

Happy reading!

Jules

TO TAME
A COWBOY

JULES BENNETT

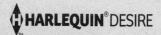

Special thanks and acknowledgment to
Jules Bennett for her contribution to the
Texas Cattleman's Club: The Missing Mogul miniseries.

Recycling programs
for this product may
not exist in your area.

ISBN-13: 978-0-373-73277-7

TO TAME A COWBOY

Printed in U.S.A.

Books by Jules Bennett

Harlequin Desire

Her Innocence, His Conquest #2081
Caught in the Spotlight #2148
Whatever the Price #2181
Behind Palace Doors #2219
Hollywood House Call #2237
To Tame a Cowboy #2264

Silhouette Desire

Seducing the Enemy's Daughter #2004
For Business...or Marriage? #2010
From Boardroom to Wedding Bed? #2046

Other titles by this author available in ebook format.

JULES BENNETT

National bestselling author Jules Bennett's love of story-telling started when she would get in trouble as a child and would tell her parents her imaginary friends were to blame. Since then, her vivid imagination has taken her down a path she'd only dreamed of. And after twelve years of owning and working in salons, she hung up her shears to write full-time.

Jules doesn't just write Happily Ever After, she lives it. Married to her high school sweetheart, Jules and her hubby have two little girls who keep them smiling. She loves to hear from readers! Contact her at authorjules@gmail.com, visit her website, www.julesbennett.com, where you can sign up for her newsletter, or send her a letter at P.O. Box 396, Minford, OH 45653. You can also follow her on Twitter and join her Facebook fan page.

First I have to thank Charles Griemsman,
editor extraordinaire, for his cheering and guidance
as we worked together on Piper and Ryan's story.

Second, to Shannon Taylor. *Thank you* doesn't cover
all you did to help me. From reading my rough draft to
talking me through scenes over the phone to making
sure I had my cowboy "lingo" down correctly. :-)

And last, to the other amazing authors
in this continuity. I had a blast swapping scenes
and getting inside your heads for a bit!

Prologue

Twenty Years Ago

Piper Kindred was so sick of being snubbed by the girls who thought the only things worth talking about were their lip gloss shades and where they got their new outfit. She was also sick of being disrespected by the boys who didn't quite know how to handle her so they just ignored her.

Where did she fit in? God, she hated school. Even the third grade sucked. She'd switched schools so she didn't have friends yet, but seriously, if this was how the rest of the year would go, she'd rather be home riding her horse or learning to rope. School was overrated anyway.

Especially considering that at recess for the past two days all she'd heard were brats mocking her. Today was no different.

"Look at her belt buckle."

"What kind of name is Piper, anyway?"

"Dude, did you see that clown hair?"

Piper rolled her eyes at the annoying kids trying to get on her nerves. It was working, but she'd never let them know it.

She'd heard enough crap from other kids about her name and her wardrobe. So she liked plaid flannel and cowgirl boots; she was Walker Kindred's daughter. Didn't they know he was a legend? Morons. Didn't even know her father was pretty much a celebrity.

And the hair comments they kept tossing her way? Yeah, there was hardly a day that went by she didn't have to hear something about "carrot top" or "finger in a light socket" or "Bozo the Clown." So it was red and curly. To be honest, she liked being different from all these other stupid kids.

"Don't let them get to you."

Piper spun around on the playground. A boy at least a head taller than her stood with his thumbs hanging in his belt loops. He had a head full of messy dark brown hair and the brightest blue eyes she'd ever seen. And he was wearing a flannel shirt. Obviously they were the only two cool kids.

"I'm not letting them get to me," she told him, lifting her chin in defiance. "I don't care about those smelly boys or this dumb school."

He laughed. "My name is Ryan Grant. Thought you could use a friend if you were tired of playing alone."

"Yeah, well, I'm not. Those losers have no idea how awesome this belt buckle is," she told the boy. "My dad got it for me when he won the PRCA title last year."

The boy stepped forward, his brows raised. "Your dad won the PRCA title?"

"Yeah."

He shook his head. "You don't have to lie to make friends."

Piper shoved her hands onto her hips and glared at the annoying kid. "I don't have to lie at all because my father is the coolest man ever. There's not a bronc he can't ride."

Okay, probably there was, but still. Her dad was the coolest and he got paid for riding and being a cowboy. Could any of those other loser kids say that?

"What's your dad's name?" Ryan asked, obviously still skeptical.

"Walker Kindred."

Ryan laughed. "You're lying."

"I don't care what you think. My name is Piper Kindred and Walker is my father. Like you know anything about the rodeo anyway. You probably don't even know what PRCA stands for."

"Professional Rodeo Cowboys Association," he shot back. "And I know who Walker Kindred is."

"Then why do you say I'm lying?"

"Because, well…you're a girl. I've never seen a girl who knows about the rodeo."

Why were boys so dumb? For real?

Piper sighed, so ready to be done with recess and get back inside where she could just concentrate on her schoolwork and get another miserable day behind her.

"Whatever," she told him, rolling her eyes. "I don't care what you think if you're going to be just as stupid as the others."

He crossed his arms over his chest and grinned. "Okay, since you got to ask me a rodeo question, I get to ask you one. I bet you can't answer it."

Piper had had enough. She clenched her fist and plowed it into his nose. When he landed on his butt on the blacktop, she loomed over him.

"I don't have time for jerks who think I'm lying," she told him. "I've grown up around the circuit. Walker is my father and if you have any more stupid things to say, I have another fist waiting on you."

Ryan shook his head and came back to his feet. Surprisingly, he was grinning.

"You pack a mean punch, even if you are a girl."

Piper eyed him. Apparently that was a compliment.

"You wanna hang after school?" he asked, holding his hand to his nose then looking at it to see if he was bleeding.

Piper figured they'd just made some sort of bond so she nodded. "Sure, but don't think just because I'm a girl that I don't know everything about the rodeo."

Ryan laughed. "Wouldn't dream of it, Red."

She sighed and headed toward the double doors as the bell rang for them to go back inside.

If the worst he called her was Red, he might just become her one and only friend.

One

Piper Kindred did a double take at the black sports car. Her heart sank, bile rising in her throat. No, it couldn't be.

Oh, sweet mercy. There was no way this massive accident would have no casualties. Wreckage lay crushed with mangled pieces across the median, shattered glass scattered along the stretch of highway, a black BMW on its top and a large tractor-trailer on its side, blocking both lanes of traffic.

As a paramedic, Piper had seen plenty of wrecks, fatalities and gut-wrenching scenes, but nothing settled fear as deep within her as seeing the familiar car that was so often in her driveway...the car that belonged to her best friend, Ryan Grant.

The ambulance barely came to a stop before Piper grabbed her heavy red medical bag, hopped out and hit the ground running. The warm November sun beat down on her back as she ran toward the chilling scene.

The medic in her couldn't get to the victims fast enough. The woman in her feared what she'd uncover once she reached Ryan.

Once closer, she squatted in an attempt to see the inside of the vehicle. A wave of relief swept through her the second she realized the car was empty. Okay, so he wasn't trapped, but what was the extent of his injuries?

Sirens blared in near surround sound between the police, ambulances and a fire truck trying to assist the wounded and clean up the mess.

Piper tried to keep her eye out for Ryan, hoping she'd see him sitting in the back of an ambulance with just an ice pack on his head. But her duty was to assist where needed…not to seek out those most important in her life.

As she moved closer to the tractor-trailer, where the majority of the cops seemed to be congregated, she noticed numerous Hispanic people huddled together. With disheveled clothes, scraggly beards and various cuts and bruises, Piper couldn't help but wonder what they were all doing at the scene of an accident involving only one semi and the car of her best friend.

Piper ran to the group of obviously injured men and women. Some were crying, some had their heads dropped between their shoulders and some were shouting Spanish slang even she didn't understand because of the rapid rate, but she could tell they were angry and scared.

As Piper passed two uniformed police officers she heard the words *illegal* and *FBI*. Yeah, this was so much more than an ill-fated accident. By the number of uniformed officers scouring the area, it looked as though these people were not here legally.

Moments later she heard other officers discussing how so many stowaways were hidden in such a small compartment in the back of that semi. This situation was beyond what Piper was used to. Her job right now was to assess and treat the victims, not to worry about the legalities of this mess.

"Where do you need me?" she asked another paramedic who was examining a man's leg beneath his torn pants.

"The truck driver was pretty shaken," the paramedic told her. "He's sitting in the back of a squad car for questioning right now. No visible injuries, but his pupils were dilated and he did say his back was hurting. Seems he was driving this illegal group and he had no clue."

Piper nodded, gripped her bag tighter and headed toward the squad car closest to the overturned semi. Sure enough a trooper had his forearm resting on the roof of the car as he leaned in and listened to whatever the man seated in the back was saying.

"I swear I had no clue what was in the back of my truck. Please, you've got to believe me," the driver pleaded. "I was just trying to get into the other lane and that car came out of nowhere. I didn't see him at all."

According to the man's story, he was completely innocent. This was a mess of epic proportions and not something a few questions would solve. But all Piper needed to do was to assess the man to see if he needed to go to the hospital or if he could continue being questioned.

"Officer, may I please check him out?" Piper asked. "I understand he has back pain."

The officer stood to his full height and nodded, but didn't move too far away. Often medics and cops worked together. Being a first responder required teamwork and so far she'd never had an issue with any cop getting in the way of her treating a patient at the scene.

Piper leaned in and saw a middle-aged man with a protruding belly hanging over his faded jeans, a dirty, bushy blond mustache with matching beard and nicotine-stained fingers.

"Sir, my name is Piper and I'm an EMT. I was told your back is hurting. Can you stand?"

He nodded and slid out of the car as Piper backed up. When he came to his full height, he winced, grabbing his lower back—whether for show to get the officer's sympathy or because the pain was indeed real, she didn't know. Yet again, not her place to judge.

"If you'll come this way, we can set you in the back of an ambulance. You may want to go to the hospital just to make sure nothing else is wrong, but I can get your vitals over here."

"I appreciate that, ma'am."

As she led the man toward the nearest empty ambulance, her eyes scanned the crowd for Ryan. Had he already been taken to the E.R.? Were his injuries life-threatening? The unknowns were killing her.

She knew a life flight chopper hadn't been dispatched to the scene, so that was a mild comfort. Not only for the fact Ryan didn't need a medevac, but that none of the others involved in the accident did, either.

Another ambulance arrived on the scene as Piper assisted the truck driver into the back of a vacant one. When fresh paramedics hopped from their emergency vehicle and made their way toward the group of injured people, she jogged back over to assist.

But froze in her tracks as one head lifted and a familiar set of dark eyes met hers. He was amid a group of Mexicans, but this man... She knew this man.

Dear God. How could this... What the hell...?

"Alex?" she whispered to herself.

Piper took off at a dead run and stopped beside Alex Santiago. Her bag dropped at her feet as she held her breath.

Was she honest to God seeing the man who'd disappeared months ago without a trace? Could it truly be him?

The man glanced up at her, holding his hand over his eyes to block the glaring afternoon sun.

My God. It *was* him. The hair was a shaggy, unkempt mess and the scruff on his cheeks and chin indicated he hadn't shaved in a few days or even weeks. But this was Alex… The man who'd been missing from Royal, Texas, for months.

The man most people assumed had become a victim of foul play, maybe even at his best friend's hand. But here he was, living and breathing.

"Alex, what on earth are you doing here? Where have you been?" she asked, eyeing the knot on the side of his head.

He winced as she slid her fingertip over the swollen bump. "You must have me confused with someone else. My name isn't Alex."

Piper's hand stilled above his head as she leaned down to look him in the eyes. She was pretty sure she knew what her friend looked like. Just because she hadn't seen him in months didn't mean she was clueless.

She looked closer. Um…yeah, this was Alex. If he didn't think he was Alex, then he'd hit his head too hard in that crash. But at least he was alive.

"Your name is Alex Santiago," she told him, making sure to keep her eyes locked on to his, waiting for a spark of recognition from his end.

His brows drew together and he slowly shook his head. "I've never heard that name."

"Then what do people call you?" she asked, worry growing deeper with each passing moment.

Alex's eyes searched hers; he opened his mouth, closed it and sighed. "I don't…remember. That doesn't make sense. How could I not know my own name?"

"You have a good bump here on your head," she reminded him as her eyes traveled down to the wrist he cradled in his other hand. "Looks like you may have broken your wrist."

He glanced down and simply nodded. Piper worried

shock may be setting in. Between the accident and the apparent memory loss, she had no doubt Alex was shaken.

"Let's get you to an ambulance and see what the doctors have to say once you get to the hospital," she said gently. "I'm sure you'll remember you're Alex Santiago in no time. I'm Piper Kindred and we've been friends for a while. Can you at least tell me how you got into that truck?"

Piper lifted her duffel bag, helped Alex to his feet and held an arm around his waist when he started to sway. "Easy," she told him. "No rush. We're only going to that ambulance a few feet away. Think you can make it or should I bring a gurney?"

"No, I'm okay."

She didn't quite believe him so she kept him leaning against her side as she led him to the waiting ambulance.

"Go ahead and lie down on that cot," she said as she assisted Alex into the back of the vehicle.

"Do you know where you are?"

His blank look added to the sickening feeling in her stomach.

"We ready to roll?"

Piper glanced at the other EMT on the scene. They might as well go without her because there was no way in hell she was leaving without at least seeing that Ryan was okay…and to tell him of miraculously discovering Alex.

"Go ahead and take him. He's got some memory loss so he doesn't know his name. Make sure the doctors are aware this is Alex Santiago and he's been missing for months. I'll go inform an officer because Alex was the subject of an ongoing investigation."

Turning her attention back to Alex, Piper offered a warm smile. "You're in good hands now, Alex. I know you're confused, but I'll be at the hospital as soon as I can to check on you."

Continuing to hold on to his wrist, Alex leaned back on the gurney. Piper closed the doors and tapped the back to inform the driver he was good to go.

With several paramedics now on the scene, Piper felt comfortable going in search of Ryan.

After searching frantically, running through the chaos, she found him next to the road on the other side of the overturned semi. Her knees weakened with relief at the sight of Ryan whole and upright. He was a good bit from his car, so she had to assume the officer had taken him aside to get his statement.

But glancing at Ryan and actually talking to him were two different things. He looked fine, but looks, as she'd discovered numerous times over the years, could be deceiving. Internal injuries were nothing to mess around with and could prove fatal even when a patient looked perfectly fine.

Added to needing to know the extent of his injuries, she had to tell him about the mind-blowing discovery she'd just made.

Alex Santiago was alive. Their friend who had been missing for months was alive and on his way to Royal Memorial Hospital with an obvious broken wrist and some memory loss. But he was alive.

But, my God, what in the world had he been doing in the back of a semi-truck filled with illegal Mexicans? So many questions whirled around in her mind. She had no idea what the hell was going on, but she knew Alex was probably scared and confused.

As Piper moved closer, she noticed Ryan holding on to one of his sides. A trooper was jotting down notes and nodding as he took Ryan's statement. Piper closed the gap, but stayed a few feet away, waiting for him to finish.

The sight of him with a slight bruise over his right brow

and his hair even messier than usual made Piper want to throw her arms around his broad, muscular body and squeeze him to death for scaring her. But he'd probably laugh at her if she got all misty-eyed or mushy right now.

She'd seen this cowboy compete on the rodeo circuit countless times. She'd seen him get knocked around, bucked and nearly trampled, but nothing had terrified her more than the sight of his totaled car.

The trooper stepped away and Piper inched closer on still shaky legs.

Ryan caught her eye and offered that crooked smile. "Hey, Red."

That smile could melt the panties off any woman… and it had according to rumor. But Ryan was her friend so her panties had stayed in place over the years. Though she wasn't blind—her bestie was the sexiest cowboy she'd ever laid eyes on.

With that dark, messy hair usually hidden by a black Stetson and heavy-lidded baby blues, yeah, Ryan Grant was one very fine-looking cowboy and he did some mighty nice things to a pair of well-worn jeans.

"You need to be seen," she informed him, raking her eyes over him to look for other visible injuries. "And I won't take no for an answer."

"I'm just sore and banged up a little, that's all." He reached out, grabbed one of her shaky hands and squeezed. "You look tense. I'm fine, Piper."

"You will be checked out because you'll want to come to the hospital anyway when I tell you who I saw."

Ryan shrugged, hissing and grabbing his side again. "Who?"

Piper's eyes darted down to his ribs. "If they're not broken, they're bruised, so you'll be going straight to X-ray when you get there, big boy."

"Who did you see?" he insisted.

All joking aside, she leaned in and said, "Alex."

"Alex?" he repeated. "Alex Santiago?"

Piper nodded. "He was in the back of that semi."

"Piper..." He eyed her as though she was the one who'd hit her head. "Alex was in the truck?"

She merely nodded, crossing her arms and silently daring him to argue.

"How in the hell did he get there?" Ryan asked.

Piper nodded toward another ambulance and guided Ryan toward the open back. "He doesn't remember."

Ryan, still holding his side, put his foot on the back step. "He doesn't remember how he got into the semi?"

"He doesn't remember anything," she whispered. "He didn't even know his damn name was Alex when I was talking to him. He didn't recognize me and he was totally clueless."

"Damn it." Ryan glanced around at the group of Mexicans being tended to by EMTs and talked to by the cops. "He has amnesia?"

Piper shrugged. "I honestly don't know. He had a good-size knot on his head, but that could've happened from the accident. He's on his way in the squad I came with, so we'll catch a ride with another. Right now I think we both need to get to the hospital for multiple reasons."

"I don't need to get checked out, but I'll appease you only because I want to see Alex for myself."

Piper studied him, as if she could see beyond the surface and actually make an official diagnosis.

"You all right?" he asked. "You look a little pale."

Piper caught his worried gaze and smiled. "I'm fine. And if the doctors give you the go-ahead and release you, I'm going to kick your rear end for worrying me to death when I saw your overturned car."

Ryan's wide, signature smile spread across his face. "There's that Piper love. Come on. Let's get to the hospital."

"Oh, God, Ryan." She held a hand on his arm before he could step into the back of the ambulance. "What about Cara? Someone needs to call her."

Piper couldn't even imagine what Alex's fiancée, Cara Windsor, would think when she was told he was alive. Piper was stunned and thrilled, but she was worried about how extensive this memory loss was.

"Let's get the facts from the doctor first," Ryan suggested. "We can't have her running all in there in hysterics and shock. We need to prepare her for this and have concrete information."

Piper nodded. "I agree. Let's get to the hospital. And while you're getting checked out, I'll find out Alex's status."

"Red—"

She held up a hand. "The fact my heart rate is still out of control after not knowing if you were okay or not gives me the right to override anything you say. Now get your butt in and let's get to the hospital."

Two

"Nothing broken."

Piper stood inside the thin white curtain separating Ryan's cubicle from the rest of the Emergency Room.

She crossed her arms and smiled. "Anything else you want to tell me?"

Ryan shrugged. "Not really."

Narrowing her eyes, she stalked forward. "Keeping the bruised ribs and concussion to yourself?"

Busted.

"I'm fine," he assured her. "Nothing a little over-the-counter pain meds won't fix or a good shot of my grandpa's bourbon. A cure-all, he always claimed."

Piper rested her hands on her hips, pulling the buttons across the chest of her cute little EMT uniform. Damn, but she was pretty when she was angry or about ready to light into him like some mother hen.

"You have a concussion, Ryan. No drinking."

"You medical types always take the fun out of healing."

As he'd intended, she took his joke and rolled her eyes with a hint of a grin.

"Seriously, I've had way worse getting bucked off a horse."

"You're staying at my place tonight," she told him, pointing her finger at his chest. "No arguing."

As if he'd turn down that invitation. Piper wasn't only his best friend, but a friend with whom he'd always wanted more. Yeah, he may have a concussion from that accident, but he wasn't dead.

He'd never pursued anything beyond friendship with her for a couple of reasons, the main ones being he was always traveling and she'd never shown any interest in him on an intimate level.

Added to that, her father had been a rodeo star and he'd heard Piper swear on more than one occasion that she'd never, ever fall for a cowboy.

But he was home now and ready to see if something beyond friendship could exist.

"Fine, I'll let you pamper me. But only if you'll make that chicken soup I love so much."

Piper threw her arms in the air and sighed. "Don't milk this, Ryan."

He laughed and extended his hand for her to take. She moved closer and he wasn't about to mention the trembling he instantly felt when they connected.

"Tell me about Alex," he said, stroking her palm with his thumb. "What are the doctors saying? Did you call Cara?"

Piper eased a hip onto the edge of his very narrow, very thin E.R. mattress. "The doctors are still unsure as to whether or not the amnesia was caused before or during the accident. He has old bruises, so he was in a fight or some other accident before today. His wrist has several breaks and he'll be going to surgery soon to repair that. More than likely they'll either do a plate or at the very least pins."

Broken bones were reparable, death was not. Ryan couldn't even believe that Alex was here after all these months of wondering what had happened—whether he'd run away or been the victim of foul play. But now he was back and hopefully this amnesia was short term so he could explain just what the hell had happened.

"What about Cara?" he asked.

"I just checked with the nurse and Cara has been notified. I'm sure she's on her way."

"What did they tell her?"

Piper looked down at their joined hands. "That Alex was found alive, but he'd been in an accident. He has some memory loss and a broken wrist."

"She's got to be worried sick," Ryan said.

"I can't even imagine."

"When can I get out of this bed?" Ryan grumbled. "I want to go see Alex and I think someone should be with Cara when she arrives. They're going to need their friends."

Piper nodded. "Dr. Meyers said you were free to go as long as someone stays with you overnight. I assured him you would be in good hands."

Ryan only wished he'd end up in her hands. But, alas, Piper would never see him as anything other than her best friend. Even if she did have deeper feelings, the woman was stubborn and because her father had pretty much abandoned his family to dominate the rodeo circuit, Piper would never turn to a cowboy for any kind of a relationship beyond friendship.

And that left him out, considering he'd traveled the circuit for years and now intended to open a school for children to teach them his love of rodeo. The new ranch he'd purchased a few months ago just outside town had a vast amount of acreage, perfect for teaching young children the basics and allowing them to progress to higher levels of learning all in one location.

But as much as he loved his sprawling new ranch, he

was more than willing to go to the small bungalow Piper was renovating.

"Let's get to Alex's room," he told her as he eased off the bed, concentrating on his movements so he didn't get dizzy, stumble and cause Piper to have him admitted. "Is he still in the E.R. or in his own room?"

"They just put him in a room and they're going to do the surgery in a few hours once the surgeon is available and up to speed on what happened. They have to be careful with the anesthesia because of his head trauma."

Piper slid the curtain aside with a swish and took off down the hall toward the elevators before she froze and turned back to him.

"Sorry, Ryan," she said as she waited for him to catch up. "I'm so used to going at lightning speed, I wasn't thinking you're probably sore."

"I'm fine, Red." Though he wasn't going to object when she slid her arm through his to guide him. Not that he needed it, but he appreciated her care. "I've been through worse with my job."

They reached the elevator and rode up in silence. When the doors slid open, he let Piper take the lead because she knew the hospital better than he did and he wanted her to think she was actually assisting him in walking, though he really wasn't in all that much pain except for the ribs.

"He's in the last room on the right," Piper said as they rounded the corner. "Should we both go in or just one at a time? I don't want to bombard him or overwhelm him since he won't remember us."

Ryan held on to his sore side. "He's already talked to you and I don't think I'm that intimidating."

Piper nodded. "Just don't pressure him about details. The doctors said the memories need to come naturally and not be forced."

Ryan pushed the door open and gestured for Piper to enter first.

"Hi, Alex," she greeted with a warm, kick-in-the-gut smile. "I wanted to check on you and I brought another one of your friends."

"The police just left," he told her. "I didn't know if they were going to let visitors in or not."

"I'm sure visitors are fine," she told him, stepping aside so Alex could get a look at Ryan. "And I'm sure in no time you'll be mobbed. You've had a lot of people worried to death about you."

Alex's dark eyes darted from Piper to Ryan, then back to Piper.

"Do you remember him?" Piper asked hopefully. "You guys are in the Texas Cattleman's Club."

"Sorry." Alex shook his head. "I'm afraid I don't."

"It's okay. I'm Ryan Grant."

Ryan stepped toward the bed and still couldn't believe his eyes. Alex truly was here. He was banged up and in desperate need of a haircut and shave, but the man some feared dead was actually alive.

"I think we should also tell you that someone else is coming to see you," Piper said. "Cara Windsor."

Ryan watched Alex for any sign of recognition. But nothing. Not a blink, not even an eye twitch.

"She's your fiancée," Ryan stated. "But if you're not ready to see her, that's fine. She'll do whatever you want."

"I felt she deserved to know you were alive," Piper told Alex.

Alex leaned his head back against the stark white pillow. "Damn it. This is frustrating. I don't even recognize my own fiancée's name? What the hell happened to me?"

Piper patted his uninjured arm. "That's what we'll find out. Don't push it, Alex. The memories will return. The doctors still aren't sure if the memory loss is long or short term, but we will do everything we can to make sure you get your life back."

"Would you rather we ask Cara to stay out right now?" Ryan asked. "Visitors are up to you. Whatever you're comfortable with."

Alex brought his tired gaze back to Ryan. "No. No. If seeing her will help trigger something, I'm all for it. Does she know about my condition?"

"The nurse who called Cara filled her in." Piper slid her hands into the pockets of her navy work pants. "I'm sure she'll be here anytime. Is there anything you want me to get you? How's the pain?"

"The wrist hurts, but it's tolerable since they gave me some pain meds when I got here."

"Have you had any spark of a memory?" Ryan asked, coming to stand at the end of the bed.

"Nothing. I keep waiting for something... Anything." Alex glanced at Piper. "So my name is Alex..."

"Santiago," she supplied.

"And I have a fiancée?"

Piper nodded. "Cara Windsor."

Ryan waited, but thankfully Piper didn't mention any more about Cara or her father who wasn't too keen on the idea of his baby girl's engagement to Alex.

Alex may be a venture capitalist, investor and new member of the most elite men's club in the U.S., but being a member of the Texas Cattleman's Club still didn't mean he was good enough for Cara...according to her father anyway.

Alex looked at Ryan. "And you say we're members of some club?"

"The Texas Cattleman's Club," Ryan confirmed. "Do you recall any of the men there? Chance McDaniel or Gil

Addison? Chance is your good friend and Gil is the TCC president."

Alex ran a hand down his face. "I don't know either of those names."

Frustration hung heavy in the air and Ryan's heart ached for his friend. So many people cared about Alex and would want to help him through this tough time, but would Alex want a bunch of strange faces all up in his business right now?

"Oh, God."

At the veiled whisper, Piper and Ryan turned to the door to see Cara—pale face, hand covering her mouth, eyes wide. As if she realized there was an audience, she dropped her hand, straightened her shoulders and moved in with slow, easy steps, all the while never taking her eyes off the patient.

Ryan watched as Piper stepped aside and made room at the edge of the bed for Cara. Cara started to reach for Alex's hand, but stopped as if she remembered he had no idea who she was to him.

"I can't believe this," she said, her voice thick with emotion. "I've prayed for so long. Wanted to believe you were okay, but not knowing…"

Alex studied her. "Cara?"

"Yes." She held up her hand, the one showcasing an impressive diamond. "I never took it off, never gave up hope."

Ryan stepped around the bed and tapped on Piper's arm, nodding toward the door.

"We're going to let you two talk," Piper told Alex and Cara. "It's good to have you back, Alex."

He smiled and nodded, but kept his eyes locked on Cara. Hopefully seeing the love of his life would spark something that mere friends couldn't conjure up from whatever depth of suppressed memories he had.

"Call me if you need anything," Piper whispered to Cara.

"Can I talk to you for just a second?" Cara asked.

Piper nodded and stepped outside the doorway.

"Is there anything you can tell me about his status?" Cara pleaded.

"All I know is that he was found in the back of a semi in a hidden compartment with a group of illegal immigrants. The doctor isn't sure if his memory loss is from the accident or something that happened before. That's really all I know."

Cara let out a shaky breath. "Thank you for being here for him until I got here."

Piper reached out and squeezed Cara's hand. "I know we don't know each other that well, but please, if you need anything at all, I'm here. It's no comparison, but Ryan was in the accident, too, and seeing him there really shook me up. I can't imagine how you're feeling. So if you need to talk, cry or just vent, I'm here."

Cara's smile reached her watery eyes. "I appreciate that, Piper. More than you know. And I may take you up on it. I need to get back inside."

Piper gave her a brief hug and watched Cara go back on the other side of the privacy curtain just inside the door. Seconds later Ryan walked out.

Ryan closed the door to give the newly reunited couple some much needed privacy.

"Did you see his face?" Piper asked. "He looked so lost, so confused."

Ryan leaned against the door and stared up at the ceiling. "I can't even imagine what he's feeling. But they're strong. Cara will help him through this."

"But what if he doesn't remember and he doesn't love her anymore?" Piper asked.

Glancing back down, Ryan shook his head. "That won't

happen. Alex is stubborn and a fighter. He won't give up until he finds his way back to us…and Cara."

Piper looped her arm around his and tugged him away from the door as she started walking down the hall. "I hope so. But for now, they have each other and I plan on getting you home so you can rest."

"And while I rest, you'll make that chicken noodle soup?"

Piper glanced up at him, trying to hold back a smile and failing. "Only because I'm so thankful you're alive and I know how much worse you could've been injured. But don't expect this every time we're together, big boy."

"Wouldn't dream of it, Red. Wouldn't dream of it."

Three

Piper got Ryan settled on the couch, remote in hand and feet propped up, before she went to make his precious soup.

Wasn't that just like a man? Fondling the remote, reclined in a cushy chair and waiting on supper? She smiled as she headed to the kitchen. For some reason catering to Ryan didn't bother her in the least. She knew he was no slacker when it came to work. The man was iconic in the rodeo circuit and now he was working his butt off trying to get a school open for children to learn the tricks of the trade. Piper was proud of her best friend and if the man wanted chicken noodle soup, then that's what he'd get. And she'd throw in some homemade bread just because she was still so relieved he hadn't come out any worse for the wear from that scary accident.

The look of despair on Cara's face kept filling Piper's head. Cara's world had been turned upside down months ago when Alex had disappeared and again today when Cara discovered he was alive…but he wasn't the Alex she knew and loved.

Piper was grateful Ryan was in her living room, fully aware of everything and everyone around him. Not that Piper and Ryan had the romance Cara and Alex did, but the bond she shared with Ryan was the most secure relationship she'd ever had…and stronger than most marriages.

Sighing, Piper focused on the task at hand. She was thankful that when she cooked, she planned ahead and froze things. She pulled open her freezer drawer and took out the chicken and stock she'd cooked and frozen just last week.

In no time the kitchen smelled wonderful and homey, nothing a scented candle could provide.

The TV blared in from the living room and Piper smiled. He was watching bull riding and cheering like some men do with football or basketball. Her Ryan was bulls, horses and broncs all the way, baby.

She rested her palms on the edge of the granite counter and sighed as she closed her eyes and thanked God for so many things today. First, she was beyond relieved that Alex was alive and, for the most part, unharmed. Second, she was grateful nobody had been killed in that horrendous accident. But more than anything, she was beyond grateful Ryan was okay. Not only was he okay, he was dominating her television and recliner, and that was just fine with her.

If she ever decided to settle down and marry, Ryan Grant held all the right qualifications. Oh, she'd never put the moves on her best friend. That would be weird... wouldn't it?

She'd be lying if she didn't admit she used to wonder "what-if," but Ryan never saw her as more than just one of the guys. So that was the role she stuck with.

Besides, even though he had stepped aside from the rodeo circuit, he still had that thrill for adventure and danger in his blood. She couldn't live with that, not again. She'd spent years watching her mother suffer while her father chased danger on the circuit. Injury after injury, her mother swore she couldn't handle it anymore.

And finally one day, she didn't. They'd divorced and

Piper had rarely seen her father again. She refused to do that to herself or her future children.

So, while she may be looking for a man just like Ryan Grant, there was no way she could make him Mr. Right. But having him for a friend was one of the best things that had ever happened to her.

"Hey."

She turned to see Ryan, arms crossed over his chest as he leaned against the doorframe. Sweat beaded on his forehead.

Of all the times for a heat wave to sweep through Royal, Mother Nature decided now would be a good time. What happened to the cold spell they'd just had last month?

"Sorry about the air," she told him. "Remodeling your own house can save a bunch of money, but there are certain drawbacks. I'm hoping to have the system put in next week. That's why I keep the blinds down and fans on in every room. I also wasn't expecting the temperatures to get back up to Hades levels this time of year."

"I'm good," he told her. "I'm more concerned about dinner."

He smiled, but all Piper could think about was how he'd been flipped in his car only hours ago. Yet here he stood in her kitchen joking about the heat and dinner.

"You okay?" he asked.

Piper offered a smile. "I'm fine. Just slaving away in here while you do nothing. You were supposed to be resting in there, you know."

He pushed off the frame and eased toward her in that easy way he moved, but she figured he did it now so she wouldn't catch on to the fact he was still dizzy.

"I'm resting," he assured her.

"You're in the kitchen—that's not resting." She looked

up at him when he came to stand within inches. "I can't pamper you if you won't let me."

"Is that what you're doing?" he asked with a crooked grin. "Pampering me?"

"Not if you don't get your butt back in that recliner," she insisted, hands on her hips. "Now get out of my space so I can work."

"You're trembling, Red."

"It's out of anger," she lied. "You need to be relaxing."

He stepped forward, she stepped back. They danced until she backed up against the countertop.

"I think you're finally coming down from the adrenaline rush of your workday," he told her, holding her gaze and invading her personal space. "I think you're in here thanking God about Alex, about me."

She narrowed her eyes. "You know me too well."

He grinned, placing a hand beside her hip as he swayed slightly. "Yes, I do. And that's how I know your trembling and feistiness stems from relief. You know how this day could've ended."

Piper closed her eyes, an attempt to block out the initial images she'd conjured when she'd arrived on the scene… especially when she'd spotted his car. She'd have nightmares about that terrifying sight for weeks.

"You have no idea what went through my head when I saw your car," she whispered. "I couldn't take the time to single you out, I had a job to do and it nearly killed me."

Ryan brought up his other hand to stroke her cheek and she realized he'd wiped a tear away. She lifted her lids, found him studying her face as he eased closer.

"Nothing can keep me down, Red. I won't go out in something as trite as a car accident. I've been through a lot in my years and a flipped car is nothing."

Piper inhaled, taking in Ryan's masculine, familiar

scent. He stood so close and, not for the first time, Piper admired that stubbled chin and jawline, those broad shoulders and full lips.

Damn, she shouldn't be admiring her best friend's lips, no matter how kissable they looked.

"It's that danger you crave that scares me, Ryan." She valued their relationship and that she could be brutally honest with him. "You're so laid-back, so carefree. But when it comes to adventure, you live for it. Do you know how broken I'd be if I lost you?"

Those lips turned up as he shrugged. "Don't worry about me. I know my limits and I know how to remain in control."

His eyes darted to her mouth, then back up to her eyes as he inched forward. This time she knew he wasn't reacting from the concussion and swaying. He had genuine lust lurking in those baby blues.

"This is just both of us coming off adrenaline," she whispered. "Nothing more."

"Maybe. Maybe not."

His thumb stroked across her bottom lip and Piper forced herself not to slide her tongue out and taste him.

The timer on the oven beeped, making her jump.

She stepped aside, causing Ryan to move, as well. He shoved his hands into his pockets as if he didn't know where else to put them.

"Dinner is almost ready," she told him, yanking a drawer out to grab a pot holder. "I'll bring it to you."

She silently pleaded that he'd go back into the living room because if she turned back around and he was still there looking at her with those heavy-lidded hungry eyes, she feared she'd succumb and take what she thought he was offering. And, dear God, she'd die of humiliation if she ended up giving in only to find out he hadn't wanted intimacy.

How in the hell had they come to this point? Was it the adrenaline or had today's accident been a wake-up call? Surely he didn't feel that way toward her. They'd been friends for years and he'd never tried taking it to the next level.

But the desire in his eyes said he was ready. If this wasn't just an aftershock from the accident, she had to consider a whole new angle to their friendship.

No matter what, Piper knew she needed to keep her emotions under control. She couldn't get romantically involved with Ryan. Being best friends was as far as she could allow her heart to go.

She still had a sinking fear that he would get bored with being home for good. She knew him well enough to know that if he got restless, he'd head back out on the road, leaving her staring at his taillights.

Ryan closed the bathroom door and turned around to… Oh, for the love…

Could he not catch a damn break? First he wasn't steady on his feet because he'd hit his head, then he'd nearly kissed his best friend and now this? Come on.

Lingerie everywhere. Every damn where.

Red lace, yellow satin… Bras, thongs, silky-looking nightgowns. Of course she hung this up to dry. And of course laundry day was the day he had to stay with her.

Well played, Fate.

As if that damn near kiss in the kitchen wasn't enough to have him cursing his overactive hormones, now he was faced with the very intimate undergarments Piper slid into after a shower or before bed.

He couldn't help but imagine peeling that bright blue thong down her long, toned legs.

Who knew Piper kept such a beautiful secret beneath flannel, T's and well-worn denim?

Ryan rested his hands on the edge of the sink and stared at himself in the mirror. What the hell had he been thinking rubbing her lip like that? He knew she was leery of trusting people. After all, he'd been in her life since she'd punched him in the face in grade school for accusing her of lying about the rodeo. Of course, once he'd finally believed her dad was *the Walker* Kindred, Piper's cool status had skyrocketed. They'd been near inseparable since.

So why had he taken such a dumb, careless risk with her?

Ryan sighed, reaching to turn on the faucet to splash some cold water on his face. He'd taken a risk because he'd always wondered what that sometimes smart mouth felt like, tasted like.

Oh, they'd shared pecks on the cheek and countless hugs over the years, but Ryan fantasized about peeling back another layer, finding that hidden sexuality.

He'd been on the road so much, he'd known it wouldn't be fair to her to start a relationship. She'd lived through enough comings and goings when her parents were married. No way would Piper want to have a part-time boyfriend. But it was hell always coming home between circuit tours, seeing her, hanging out with her and not touching her.

And because they were best friends, once he'd had to hear about the night she'd lost her virginity to some schmuck who hadn't deserved her, let alone something so sacred.

Ryan splashed his face once more with the refreshing water and used the small white hand towel to dab it dry.

With his face buried in the terry cloth, Ryan inhaled her sweet, jasmine scent and groaned.

"Damn."

He was pathetic. On the circuit he could've had damn near any buckle bunny he'd wanted but, despite what the media had portrayed, he truly wasn't a man-whore. He'd had many lonely a night when he'd wonder about Piper... Wonder what she was doing or who she was with. Wonder if she was falling in love with some local cowboy who only dressed the part but played it safe or if she was cozying up with someone even calmer like a teacher or a banker.

He'd spent much of his time on the road wondering what his best friend was doing back in Royal without him.

And admitting that to even himself was a big step. For years he'd fought the growing attraction, thinking the emotions stemmed from her being the only woman he was that close to with whom he'd never slept.

But Ryan knew different. He knew Piper was special, which meant she deserved someone special who would treat her right and be the man she needed him to be. A man who would stay grounded and give her the stable life she'd always craved.

"You okay?"

Piper tapped on the door and Ryan pushed away from the sink, which he had to grab on to again because quick motions like that weren't the smartest move to make.

"I'm fine," he called back. "Be right there."

After I get my libido and dizziness in check.

He took a deep breath, wincing at the pain in his side from his damn bruised ribs. He opened the door and turned the corner, only to find himself tilting. Or was the hallway moving? Either way, before he could get a hand to the wall, he went down. Flat on his face.

"Damn it."

Piper came rushing around the corner. "Oh, Ryan. What happened?"

She squatted to take his arm and humiliation set in. Really? Was this necessary? Did he have to be coddled by the woman he'd rather be seducing?

Surely the sight of sexy lingerie hadn't caused all the blood to rush south.

"This damn concussion made me dizzy," he told her, coming to his feet. Slowly. "The last time I had a concussion, I was laid up in bed for two days."

Piper wrapped her delicate arm around his waist and smiled up at him. "And I'm sure you had some cute little buckle bunny keeping you company and playing nurse."

Ryan laughed as she led him back to the living room and into the recliner. "Nope. Just my partner, Joe, and he complained the entire time."

Above him, Piper propped her hands on her flared hips and lifted one perfectly arched brow. "I know how those hoochie mamas are. Not only are you a big name, you're smokin' hot. You should've demanded someone who looked better in a skirt."

Ryan laughed so hard, he had both hands on his side trying to suppress the pain. "Smokin' hot? You think it's wise to call me that after what almost happened in your kitchen?"

Piper shrugged. "You've seen yourself, Ryan. Don't deny it. I can admit when I think someone is sexy and there's nothing wrong with stating the truth. As for what *didn't* happen in the kitchen, I already told you, it was just adrenaline."

Ryan held her gaze, waiting on her to look away because they both knew she was lying. Adrenaline had nothing to do with the near kiss. A kiss he could practically taste.

"Stay right there," she ordered. "I'll bring you a tray with your food on it. Do you need another pain pill?"

"I'm good," he said, shaking his head. "I'll tell you if I want one later."

Her eyes narrowed. "Don't try to be macho. If it hurts, no one has to know you needed something to take the edge off."

Ryan leaned his head back against the cushiony chair and laughed. He knew exactly what would take the edge off. Unfortunately he feared she'd give him a black eye if he mentioned it.

"Whatever that smirk is, I know your mind has wandered into the gutter." Piper bent down, pointing in his face. "Don't think I don't know how your dirty little brain works."

Grinning at her, he shrugged. "And that's why you're my best friend. You know and you still love me for it."

Piper rolled her eyes and went back into the kitchen. Ryan didn't even try to look away from those swinging hips. The woman was going to be the death of him.

Unless he actually got her into bed. Because if that day ever came, Ryan knew they'd set each other on fire with all this chemistry suddenly simmering between them.

Four

Okay, so sleeping naked wasn't an option, but damn it was hot in here. Ryan had gone all the way down to his black boxer briefs, put the large box fan blowing right toward the bed and he'd kicked off all the covers. Even the ceiling fan on high wasn't helping.

Of course, it wasn't just the heat that was bothering him; it was the damn woman who insisted on pampering him. While he loved a little bedside manner now and again, he'd prefer it with a little more petting and kissing and a hell of a lot more naked skin than his nurse had showed.

Ryan tried to get comfortable, but his damn side was killing him and that embarrassing fall he'd taken earlier in the hallway hadn't helped. But he wasn't about to mention that to Piper. She'd rush him back to the E.R. for more X-rays. Surely she had some over-the-counter pain meds. Maybe that and an ice pack would help.

If she only knew half the injuries he'd had over the years, she wouldn't be so worried about a few bruised ribs and a concussion.

He glanced at the bedside clock. Nearly midnight and he hadn't heard anything in the house for a while. More than likely Piper was sleeping in something satiny, sans sheets and blankets to stay cool, with all that silky red hair spread across her pillow.

When she tapped on his door, Ryan jerked up in bed. Damn ribs had him wincing and clutching at the sheet like a baby. Obviously she wasn't resting.

"Come on in."

He had no idea what he expected her to be wearing when she stepped in, but booty shorts and a skimpy tank both in the color of a pale blue was not it. Would he have welcomed her in had he known she was wearing so little? Hell, yeah. Even if he didn't have permission to touch, he would look and capture mental picture after mental picture to use for future fantasies.

How pathetic could he be? In his defense, he usually only saw her in that ugly work uniform or denim and boots. Though he did admire her in a nice pair of fitted jeans and those sexy cowgirl boots she wore. Now if he could just get her to wear them with a little skirt or something to show off those long legs. And her pajamas did cover more than a bathing suit, but still…

"I brought you an ice pack and some ibuprofen."

With all his fantasizing, he hadn't even noticed she carried a bottle of water and ice pack in one hand and three pills in the other.

"I assumed you wouldn't come ask for anything." She set the water on the bedside table and handed him the pills. "So here they are and we can pretend you're still macho and repel pain, but humor me, take the pills and use the ice pack."

Ryan laughed, popped the pills into his mouth and took a long swig of water. He needed it to replace the saliva that had all dried up when his best friend and her smokin' hot body had sauntered in.

"To be honest, I was just thinking of getting something for the pain."

"Let me look at your ribs," she told him, easing down on the side of the bed. "I'll try not to poke too much."

While most women who wanted to get up in his business tended to tick him off, he found Piper's gentle hands and caring nature sexy and appealing. She was certainly no buckle bunny with blatant sexual advances. Piper wasn't a woman who needed to throw herself at a man to gain attention, nor did she need a man to complete her.

But that didn't mean he wouldn't try like hell to get her attention. This was new territory for him, but after seeing passion flare in her eyes in the kitchen earlier, he was confident in his quest.

Piper Kindred had been independent since she'd bopped him in the eye in the third grade and as the years had moved on, he'd respected her more and more.

But now his feelings were growing beyond respect, beyond friendship. And now that he'd retired from the circuit and was closer to opening his own rodeo school, the thought of settling down appealed to him more and more. *Piper* appealed to him more and more. He'd have to be damn sure he wanted to cross over that friendship line and take her along for the ride.

As she slid her hands over the tattoos covering his torso and side, Ryan resisted the urge to reach out and move a wayward curl that had slid down over her eye. Instead he allowed his gaze to journey down to the vee of her cami. The thin material did nothing to hide the outline of her nipples. And those dainty straps could be snapped off with one expert flick of his fingers.

"There's still some swelling," she murmured. "But the ibuprofen and the ice will help with that."

She glanced up at him, and he was totally busted for looking at her chest.

"Are you serious?" she joked with a smile. "You're checking out my boobs?"

Ryan shrugged. "You put them out there."

Piper rolled her eyes. "I sleep in this, you moron. Besides, you've seen way better racks on the hoochie mamas that chase you all over the circuit. There's not a lot here to see."

"Listen, I'm a guy," he countered. "You should be worried if you'd walked in here like that and I *didn't* stare. Boobs are boobs and we want to see them all."

"Yes, I know. Any hint of skin around the chest area and you guys instantly quit blinking and your mouths fall open."

Grinning, Ryan took the ice pack she held out. "We only do that with attractive women."

"Oh, please." She laughed. "Besides, Ryan, we're best friends. I'm like one of the guys."

"Not from where I'm standing. You're all woman."

With no effort on his part, his tone had changed. His voice had deepened, his smile had faded. Yeah, he wasn't kidding about her not being just one of the guys. Yes, she'd grown up around cowboys and now worked with mostly men, but she was far from a guy and all that silk and lace hanging to dry in her guest bath proved his point.

"You've seen me in a swimsuit," she reminded him, her voice softer. "It's not a big deal."

He couldn't stop his eyes from roaming over her bare skin and that valley between her breasts. When he met her gaze again, he didn't see desire as he'd hoped, he saw uncertainty.

"You must've really hit your head," she joked. "You've never talked like this before or looked at me like…like…"

"Like what?" he murmured.

"Like you want me."

"I know exactly what I'm saying and what I want, Piper." He purposely let his eyes drop to her mouth as he slid his hand up and over her bare shoulder. "You know how special you are in my life and how much I value our friendship."

"Then why are you looking at me like you want to kiss me?" she whispered.

"Because I do."

She didn't back away, but her body froze beneath his touch. The dead last thing he wanted to do was to scare her or to make her uncomfortable. Unfortunately he'd managed to do both.

His plan of seduction needed a bit more work. He wasn't used to being the one chasing. If he didn't botch it, this could be interesting.

Ryan dropped his arm and eased back into his propped-up pillows. "Thanks for the pills and the ice."

Her brows pulled together. "So you get all worked up and then…nothing?"

Shrugging, Ryan grinned. "I've been worked up before, Red. Now get out of here before I take what I really want."

Deep green eyes widened, but she just nodded as she came to her feet. "Good night, Ryan. I'll be in periodically to check on you."

He swallowed, afraid that if he opened his mouth, he'd beg her to stay, to crawl beneath the sheets with him and see just how far they could push their friendship.

But in the end he watched her go, and waited for the door to click shut before he groaned out his frustration.

Thank God his injuries weren't worse. There was no way he could stay here long term and not want to try his hand at playing house with his very sexy, very intriguing best friend.

And he'd been scared that retirement would be boring.

* * *

Mercy. Someone had beaten him with a two-by-four…
or his car had flipped and pinned him. Either way, Ryan
nearly whimpered when he crawled—yes, crawled—out
of bed the next morning.

He'd been thrown from a horse countless times. But
normally he'd soaked in a tub of hot water and have a
nice rub-down after to help ease the pain that would inevitably set in.

But asking Piper for a rub-down last night would've
only ended one way…with all their clothes off.

Padding down the hallway toward the kitchen, Ryan
rounded the corner. At the small kitchen table, Piper sat
with papers spread around her and her hand holding her
forehead up while her other hand scribbled something.
A tall oscillating fan sat in the corner, rotating back and
forth to stir the air.

"Piper?"

She jerked, dropped the pencil and sent it rolling off
onto the tile. "Ryan? You okay? I didn't expect you up
this early."

Her eyes ventured down his body, heating him even
more. Okay, if she didn't keep her eyes up, she was really
going to get a sight. He was barely holding it together as
it was, considering she sat there in that damn flimsy pale
blue tank. The outline of her nipples mocked him just as
it had last night.

"I couldn't sleep, but I'm usually up early anyway."

"I know you cowboys are notorious for being early ris-
ers, but I was hoping you'd rest a bit more."

Piper came to her feet and damn that silky outfit looked
just as sexy this morning—more so since it was all rum-
pled against her body…not to mention how sexy that satin

looked lying against dewy skin. Yeah, the heat was taking its toll and he was reaping the benefits.

The curves of her perfectly shaped bottom taunted him. Ryan flexed his hands at his sides and called on his every last ounce of willpower.

She bent to retrieve the pencil and the top gaped just enough to give him even more to fantasize about. He looked away because, God help him, if he kept looking at her he was going to forget she was doing a good deed for him and totally swipe those damn papers off her table and lay her down and…

"Are you in a lot of pain?" she asked.

"Yeah." His tone sounded like sandpaper, but he couldn't even get enough saliva to swallow. "All over."

She tossed the pencil onto her pile of papers and moved across the room to open a small cabinet. She removed a bottle and popped the lid, shaking out three pills.

"Let me get you some water." She handed him the medicine and pulled a bottle of water from the fridge. "You probably need to keep some ice on those ribs, too."

While she busied herself getting his ice pack, he watched her turn into a paramedic right in front of his eyes. She was always putting others' needs first and it was apparent he'd interrupted something she was working on.

"What are all the papers?" he asked, nodded to the mess on the table.

Piper moved to his bare side and gently applied the pack. "Oh, it's nothing. Just the glamorous spreadsheets my life has been condensed to."

"What the hell do you need a spreadsheet for?" he asked, walking over to take a glance.

"I like organization," she explained. "I can't focus on my renovations and the budget if I don't have it laid out right in front of me."

Ryan fingered through a few sheets before he turned back to her. "I've told you I will gladly foot the bill for someone to come in and finish this. You don't have to drag out the process of fixing up your house."

Crossing her arms over her chest, Piper lifted her chin. "Are we seriously going to get into that again? I know you have a concussion, but surely you recall me not only saying no to your first offer, but hell no."

Ryan propped his hands on his hips, a little more than pleased when Piper's eyes drifted down. She quickly brought them back up to meet his gaze, but she'd looked enough to puff up his ego where she was concerned. Yes, he'd planted the seed and now he just needed to keep her sexual curiosity up.

"Listen, Red…" he started. "I know you have this stubborn pride, but I can afford to help. Why won't you let me? Pay me back as needed. That's fine if that's how you want it. But for heaven's sake, at least let me send someone to fix the air-conditioning."

Before I die from watching sweat trickle down that tempting valley between your breasts.

"I told you it will be installed in a couple of days."

"I can have someone out here today."

Piper rolled her eyes. "Quit steamrolling my life."

"'Steamrolling'?" he repeated. "I'm trying to make you more comfortablc."

"Really? Comfortable? Is that what you call it when you undress me with your eyes like you did last night and then admit you want to kiss me?"

Ryan raked a hand through his bed-head and sighed. "Piper—"

"Seriously, Ryan." She cut him off. "I want to chalk this up to your concussion, but I need to know what's going through that head of yours."

He moved forward, knowing he walked a fine line, but he loved a challenge. "Maybe I'm seeing my best friend in a new light. Maybe I find you more appealing than I ever thought and maybe since I've moved back for good, I find that spending more time with the one person who knows me best is just what I need."

Her eyes locked on to his, silence enveloped them, and the only noise cutting through the room was the faint ticking of the fan as it rotated.

"Ryan…" she began. "What you need is more rest because you're obviously delusional if you think we can be anything more than friends. Get that thought out of your head."

"Fine." For now. "What are your plans today?"

"I want to visit Alex, but at some point I need to run by the clubhouse. I'm supposed to replace the medical equipment in the day-care facility, but I need to see how bad the damage is. Some may be reparable."

The fact that some jerk had vandalized the Texas Cattleman's Club's new day-care facility because they didn't want women or children around was absurd. It just proved a narrow mind was behind last month's break-in.

"Need me to come along?" he offered.

"No, but you're more than welcome to come to the hospital with me if you'll put your Romeo moves on the back burner."

Ryan mock bowed. "Your wish is my command."

She twirled around and headed down the hall. In no time her door shut and he assumed she was putting clothes on. Shame that.

Ryan ran a hand down his stubbled face and grinned. There was no way he could get the thought of her and him beyond friends out of his head. He'd just gotten cozy with the idea, and the prospect of seducing his best friend was growing more and more appealing by the minute.

Especially since she'd pretty much thrown down the gauntlet. She should know him better than that. Didn't he always accept a challenge?

Ryan laughed to the empty kitchen. Retiring from the circuit and moving back to Royal was the best move he ever made.

Five

Piper drove her truck to the hospital, with her passenger pouting the whole way over the fact she'd refused his offer of money or help with her renovations.

First of all, she'd already told him no. She was more than capable of building her house with her own two talented hands and her meager savings. Yes, it would take longer, but the satisfaction she got in the end from knowing she'd done it herself would be well worth the tears, sweat and sad bank account.

Second, how in the world could she concentrate on anything when Ryan had looked at her in a whole new light last night? She'd tried to play it off, even joke about the concussion, but Piper wasn't naive or stupid. Ryan was developing feelings for her that she wasn't ready for and might never be.

Okay, so maybe he wasn't just pouting about the money.

And yes, at one time she'd wondered what-if… But the fear of losing him as a friend had overridden any lustful feelings she'd conjured.

He'd looked so damn sexy lying in her guest bed with his chest bare and the tattoos showing along his side, his pecs and one arm. Ryan Grant was truly a work of art and she might have taken her time in running her fingertips along his well-defined muscles.

"Do you think he's regained any memories?" Ryan asked as they pulled into the parking lot at Royal Memorial Hospital.

"I hope, but there's really no way of knowing." She found a spot surprisingly close to the front doors. "With his scans showing both old and new head injuries, we have no idea just what the hell he endured during those months he was missing."

Ryan sighed. "Hopefully he'll remember soon, not only for his own sanity, but for Cara and Chance."

"I know. I hope when Alex recalls what happened, that those who accused Chance of having anything to do with this come crawling to him for forgiveness."

Piper hopped out of her truck. The mere thought of Chance McDaniel, Alex's good friend, having anything to do with his disappearance was ridiculous…at least to her it was. Just because Chance and Cara used to date was no reason for Chance to try taking Alex out of the picture permanently.

Chance was an upstanding citizen, and he might still have feelings for Cara, but the man was honorable and loyal. No way would he have had Alex kidnapped.

Piper and Ryan moved through the hospital's double doors as they whooshed open. Silently they rode the elevator together and headed toward Alex's room. Tension was going to be high whether his memory was back or not. So many people were waiting on answers and watching him closely for any sign of recognition.

When they rounded the corner, Piper saw Cara at the end of the long, stark white hallway on her cell and dabbing at the corners of her eyes with a tissue.

Obviously not good news.

Piper glanced at Ryan. "Why don't you go in and see Alex? I'll wait out here and talk to Cara."

Ryan slipped into the room and Piper waited while Cara finished her call and slid the phone into her pocket.

"He still has no memory?" Piper asked, pulling Cara into a warm embrace.

"No. And Zach just left. He didn't remember his own business partner." Cara sniffed. "But I thought for sure he'd remember me…what we shared."

Piper held her friend until Cara eased back, dabbing her eyes once again.

"I'm sorry, Piper."

"Don't be sorry for me," Piper insisted, sliding Cara's honey-blond hair back off her forehead. "I'm willing to lend my shoulder anytime and I'd say if anyone deserves a good cry, it's you."

Piper couldn't imagine the emotions swirling through Cara. The woman, engaged to the love of her life, had had him taken away, and now that she had him back, had discovered he still wasn't fully hers. The nightmare for Cara continued.

"It means a lot that you care so much," Cara told her. "Alex and I both need support right now."

"Of course you do and I'm happy to be here for you," Piper replied with a smile.

"I brought some pictures this morning," Cara said, looking down at her wet tissue. "I thought seeing the happier times we shared would trigger something. But he just stared at them with a blank face and then he apologized to me. I had to step out here. I refuse to break down in front of him. He needs me strong."

"You're stronger than I could be." Piper squeezed Cara's slender shoulders. "And his love didn't die, Cara. It's still in there. We just need to give him some time. No one knows what he went through, so the doctors aren't sure how to deal with it."

Cara nodded and raised her head. "Do I have mascara under my eyes?"

Piper smiled. "No. You look beautiful as always."

"I doubt that. I'm an ugly crier, but I've been holding it together in front of Alex. Can't have him thinking I'm some sort of weak woman."

Piper laughed. "Honey, you are anything but weak. You've been through a lot these past few months. It's certainly understandable that you'd be upset now that he's back with no memory. Even Alex would understand if you had a breakdown."

Cara shook her head. "I won't break down in front of him. He needs me to help him through this. And that's exactly what I intend to do."

"Are you ready to head back in or do you need a moment?" Piper asked.

"I'm okay. He'll be happy to see someone besides me again."

"Oh, I wouldn't bet on it," Piper said, holding the door open for Cara to enter.

Alex lay in the bed, his arm now in a cast from the surgery he'd had the night before to repair his broken wrist.

With his hands in his pockets, Ryan was across the room, half sitting against the windowsill. His eyes darted to Piper and she couldn't help but feel whatever they'd started last night was far from over. The man could hold her in her place with simply one heavy-lidded gaze. How did he have such a hold over her after a few honest words? His words should've scared her to death, but instead they'd excited her. Aroused her.

God, she was in trouble here. Her stomach had never fluttered over a man before and she was even more out of her element because her hunky best friend was causing those flutters.

"Hey, Piper," Alex said, offering a brief smile. "I just told Ryan that you don't have to feel like you need to be here checking on me all the time. I'm sure you have a life. Besides, I've had several visitors. Apparently, I know a lot of people."

Piper nodded. "And all of them are worried about you. Did the doctors say anything about your amnesia?"

Alex shook his head. "I had a CAT scan, but they can't tell from that. All it showed was multiple head traumas."

"It'll come in time," she assured him, praying she wasn't lying.

"Not soon enough," he told her. "I can't imagine what you all went through."

His eyes sought Cara. The muscle in his jaw ticked as his eyes filled. "What she's been through because of me is killing me."

"I'm fine, Alex," Cara assured him. "Just concentrate on getting better. I'm not going anywhere."

Piper's throat clogged with emotions. These two were going to fight their way back to each other. As she glanced across the room, Ryan was still looking at her. The tension, the love, in this room was almost more than Piper could take.

She could not get wrapped up in that emotion called love. Look what it had done to her mother. The woman had had a marriage she'd always dreamed of to the love of her life, yet it hadn't been enough. In the end, it hadn't held together the bond of marriage.

But as Piper watched the chemistry between Cara and Alex, she couldn't help but pray that love would be enough here. These two deserved happiness, deserved to find their way back to each other.

"Is there anything we can get you guys?" Ryan asked.

"Cara, have you eaten today? Piper and I can stay while you go out for a bit."

Cara waved a perfectly manicured hand. "Oh, no. I'm fine."

"I'm fine, too," Alex declared from the bed. "I don't need babysitters."

Cara bit her lip as if to fight off tears and Piper wanted to comfort her. But Piper also understood pride was a very sacred emotion and Cara wanted to be strong in front of Alex.

"I'm sorry," Alex murmured. "It's just hell being here, not knowing what led up to this and knowing I've hurt so many people."

"You didn't hurt anyone." Ryan spoke up. "You may have developed amnesia before you vanished and wandered off. Or someone could've had a hand in your disappearance. If that's the case, then whoever is behind this is the one who hurt so many people. You just happened to be a pawn in someone's sick game."

The list of suspects was short, but Piper didn't want to believe anyone she knew and trusted could be so cold and calculating. She knew the police were thoroughly investigating everyone in Alex's life.

She was sure Chance couldn't be behind Alex's disappearance. It had to be someone else.

Alex had recently been elected into the elite Texas Cattleman's Club and most people were excited to have him as a member. Cara's dad hadn't been too thrilled, but Piper didn't think that would be grounds to have someone kidnapped. But who else could it be?

"Will you promise to call one of us if the doctors say anything more?" Piper asked Cara.

"Absolutely." Cara stepped forward and hugged Piper, whispering in her ear, "Thanks for being here."

Piper squeezed back. "I wouldn't be anywhere else."

"Alex, it's really good to have you back, man." Ryan eased around the side of the bed. "Please have Cara call me or Piper if you need anything at all. No matter how small."

Alex nodded. "Thanks. That means a lot to me."

Piper turned and nearly ran into a woman dressed in a dark gray suit. "Oh, sorry."

"No problem." The lady smiled. "I'm Bailey Collins from the Texas State Police. I've been assigned to investigate the case involving Mr. Santiago."

"I wasn't aware the state police was coming in on this," Alex chimed from his bed. "Are there leads I'm not aware of?"

Bailey's eyes darted around the room. "I'd like to speak with you alone, if I could."

"Absolutely," Piper said.

"I just need to talk to Alex for a few moments."

"We were just leaving," Ryan stated, taking Piper by the arm and leading her out the door.

"I can step outside, too," Cara added. "Take your time, Ms. Collins."

Piper and Ryan moved out into the hallway and waited for Cara to close the door behind her.

"The cops have been questioning him quite a bit," Cara told them. "They must really be onto something if they called the state investigators in. I hope they can get to the bottom of this really fast."

"They will," Ryan assured her. "We just need to support Alex and pray he gets his memory back soon."

"Do you need anything before we go?" Piper asked.

"I'm good." Cara smiled and patted Piper's arm. "You two go on. I'll call if there's any change."

Ryan hugged Cara and turned toward Piper. She slid

her arm through his as they walked away. Once inside the elevator, Piper leaned over and kissed his stubbled cheek.

"What was that for?" he asked.

"Just for being you. For being so sweet and for being alive after yesterday's accident."

His brows pulled together. "You're still shaken up over that, aren't you?"

She stared at the descending numbers above the door. "More than I wanted to admit."

Ryan kissed her on the top of her head. "That's for caring so much, Red. You'd be lost without me."

Piper laughed, elbowing him in the side. "Shut up."

Ryan gasped and grabbed hold of his ribs. "Wrong side, Red. Damn, you got them."

Piper jerked around to see him smiling.

"Kidding." He laughed. "My other side is the one that's hurt."

"I'm going to poison you next time you whine at me to make chicken soup," she joked. "Don't scare me like that again, you jerk."

Her threat didn't hold much merit considering she laughed her way through it.

He laced his fingers through hers as they stepped off the elevator. "Wouldn't dream of scaring you again."

Several days after the accident and Alex's reappearance, Ryan stepped into the Texas Cattleman's Club and took in a deep breath, which was getting easier as his bruised ribs healed.

The fact that he was now a member of one of the most elite men's clubs in all of Texas never failed to thrill him. He'd traveled all over the country competing and winning titles some cowboys only dreamed about. Since retiring and moving back to Maverick County six months ago, he'd wanted so badly to settle, to start planting roots here. What better way than to be part of a century-old club?

He'd made a name for himself on the rodeo circuit and he'd made a crap-load of money through wise investments, and he was accepted as part of this elite few.

The club was more than one hundred years old and for most of that time had seen few changes. That was, at least, until a new set of members took hold of the reins and decided to update the facilities with a tennis court and a child-care center—after they'd allowed women to become members.

And it was those decisions that had some of the long-term members sitting up a little straighter in their seats and complaining about the changes taking place to their club.

But Ryan was on board with change.

Ryan passed the old billiards room, which had been turned into the child-care facility and was now being re-paired after last month's break-in. Ryan headed to the meeting room, eager to talk to the others to get their take on Alex's return.

Ryan greeted the other members as he stepped into the room. Only five days ago Alex had been discovered and Ryan knew this meeting would be like no other they'd had thus far. Most of the other members would be excited to have Alex back.

Chance stood against the wall where various hunting plaques and trophies were displayed against dark panel-ing. Next to him was Paul Windsor, Cara's dad. The two men were in deep conversation about something and Ryan would bet his entire ranch that something was the return of Alex Santiago.

Paul had made it no secret that he wanted Chance and Cara to be together. But Cara's heart belonged to Alex…

At least that's how it had looked each time Ryan had seen her at the hospital. You couldn't fake that emotional bond.

Within minutes the members were seated around the table. The club president, Gil Addison, stood at the head of the long gleaming table and called the meeting to order.

"As I'm sure you all know, Alex Santiago was found alive a few days ago," Gil stated, looking around the table. "I went to the hospital yesterday to see him. He's suffering from amnesia. The doctors are still unsure if it's short or long term."

"So far he recognizes no one and even names aren't ringing a bell," Ryan interjected.

Paul Windsor grunted. "I haven't been, but I hear the prognosis isn't good."

Ryan listened, not a bit surprised that Paul hadn't visited Alex. Paul was one of those high-society men who felt no one was good enough for his little girl. Added to that, Alex didn't come from money—he was a self-made millionaire. Paul Windsor turned up his nose at nearly everyone, but at Alex in particular, since the younger man had his sights set on Cara.

"Actually, he was just released from the hospital and the prognosis is neither good nor bad," Ryan countered. "The doctors aren't sure if this is long-term or short-term memory loss. They're all just taking it one day at a time."

"I visited him." Chance spoke up. "He's frustrated, but he's confident he'll get his memory back. The doctors are telling him to take it easy because of the trauma to his head, but you know Alex."

Several men around the table chuckled, but Paul continued to look put off.

"Cara is pretty confident, too," Ryan added. "She's hardly left his side."

Paul's frown deepened and Ryan couldn't help but smile

inwardly. Ryan wasn't one to stir trouble, but he really didn't care for Paul Windsor. The man was arrogant and tried to rule everything and everyone by looking down his nose at them and pointing his finger, expecting people to ask "how high" when he told them to jump. Not only that, he was a notorious ladies' man and, if Ryan's count was accurate, was now searching for wife number five. That poor woman.

"Yes, Cara has been spending a great deal of time with him," Paul all but grumbled. "But you know Cara, she'll do anything to help people. I'm sure she's spending so much time with him because she wants to help jog Alex's memory."

Chance jerked his head toward Paul, and Ryan felt like he was caught at an intense tennis match with his head bobbing back and forth.

"Cara is fragile and I'm not sure she can handle all the pressure," Paul went on. "I imagine this will take its toll on her."

Ryan nearly rolled his eyes at Paul's inaccurate statement about his daughter. But when he glanced across to Chance, the man seemed intrigued as he leaned forward on the table, eyes on Paul.

"Cara is a strong woman," Chance supplied. "But this whole situation could break the strongest of people."

Ryan kept his mouth shut. He'd seen Cara, spoken with her, and he'd never seen a more determined woman... except Piper.

But, as much as he hated to admit it, Paul and Chance were right. Cara had endured a great deal of heartache, and Chance had been a source of comfort for her in Alex's absence.

Still, Ryan had seen Cara's face when she'd stepped into that hospital room for the first time. There was love in her eyes, worry and fear had been evident, as well, but Ryan thought for sure Cara and Alex would work through this.

Even though he knew never to try to get inside the female mind, Ryan couldn't help but wonder if the lovely Cara Windsor had feelings for both men.

"Alex will likely be returning to the meetings next month," Zach Lassiter said.

Ryan glanced to the end of the table where Zach sat. The self-made millionaire shared a downtown office with Alex, and Ryan knew Zach had been worried sick about Alex. They all had.

"I invited him today," Zach went on. "I offered to pick him up, but he wasn't feeling up to it. Not that I blame him… I was just thinking it might jog his memory if he was surrounded by people he used to know."

"No need to force him to come back," Paul declared. "We can carry on without him for now."

Ryan wished Paul wouldn't be so blunt about his disdain for Alex, but Paul was blunt about everything. From women to business, Paul Windsor made no secret that he always got what he wanted. And if he didn't like you, he also made no effort to hide his feelings.

As the meeting continued, Ryan couldn't help but think of Cara and Alex at the hospital. Was Cara just there out of guilt or obligation since they were engaged?

And he couldn't think of them without thinking of the way Piper had watched the reunited couple—the hope in her eyes, the soft smile that had lit up her face.

Piper might say that she had no intention of falling in love or becoming a wife, but that woman couldn't lie worth a damn. Her actions spoke volumes and it was what she *wasn't* saying that intrigued him.

Six

Piper pried the edge of her crowbar behind the next shingle and tugged until it came loose. With her gloved hand, she picked it up and sent it sailing in the direction of the small Dumpster she'd rented for this very fun occasion.

Some women chose a day at the spa; Piper chose to spend her time getting sweaty with manual labor.

Ripping off shingles before applying new? Yeah, this was just a blast. Even more so because the previous owners hadn't removed the other roof before applying this layer, so Piper was in a double bad mood. But she was eager to see her new roof installed because she'd chosen dark brown dimensional shingles that would give her little bungalow more proportion and character.

So she got excited about roofing…that didn't make her less feminine. Did it? Just because she knew her way around a ranch, had grown up wearing dusty boots and flannel as opposed to frilly dresses didn't mean she was any less female. She liked to do her own work and didn't care about the sweat and the mess.

It would be all worth it in the end…if she made it that long. Mercy, this was hard work. Piper was starting to believe that she actually worked harder on her days off than she did when she was helping to save people's lives.

Tires crunched over dirt and gravel and she glanced

over her shoulder to see who was visiting her. She should've known. Ryan was nearly her only visitor. She had a few friends, but Ryan was like the proverbial houseguest that never left. He always showed up unannounced and she loved it. Loved that they were so comfortable with each other that her house seemed like his and vice versa. Granted he'd only been back six months from the rodeo circuit, but she was at home at the ranch he'd purchased on the outskirts of town. The sprawling eight-thousand-square-foot mansion was exquisite, and the expansive lands made it the perfect place for him to open his rodeo school.

Ryan opened his truck door. "What the hell are you doing?" he asked the second one dusty boot hit the ground.

Piper kept her back to him as she pried loose another shingle. "I'm icing a cake," she called down.

"Don't be sarcastic," he yelled back.

"Then don't ask stupid questions." She tossed the shingle into the Dumpster and went to work on another. "I have another crowbar if you're here to offer your services."

"I don't have time to offer services, but I'll do the whole damn thing this weekend if you'll come down."

She laid her crowbar on the roof and eased toward her ladder. After she safely stepped onto the ground, Piper whirled around, jerked off her work gloves and crossed her arms over her chest.

"You know I'm renovating this myself and you know I need a new roof. Why are you acting all angry? Is it because you actually saw me doing the manual labor or you're afraid I'll screw it up?"

Ryan sighed. "I'm not worried you'll screw it up. You're too much of a perfectionist. I'm worried you'll get hurt. There was no one here and if you'd fallen, who would've helped?"

A bit touched by his fear for her, Piper smiled. "I'm

fine, Ryan. I've lived alone for a long time and I'm used to taking care of myself when I get hurt."

Ryan shook his head, then reached out to shove aside a stray curl that had escaped her messy ponytail. "You shouldn't have to worry about taking care of yourself."

"Because I'm a woman?" she mocked.

"No, damn it, because I care about you."

He glanced up at the roof, rested his hands on his narrow hips and sighed. His black cowboy hat shielded his eyes from the afternoon sun, but she knew those bright baby blues were taking in her work and in his mind he was calculating how he could fit this into his schedule so she wouldn't have to do it.

"I can be here on Saturday to help you with this," he told her. "I'm busy the rest of the day, and tomorrow I have a couple things in the morning to take care of."

"I work all day on the squad tomorrow," she said, refusing to allow him to take over. "I'm off Saturday. I'll probably have it done by then."

Ryan's eyes came back to hers. "Why can't you just take my damn help? You've been like this the whole time I've known you."

Piper laid a hand over her heart as if to ward off any hurt from seeping in, but he'd take her gesture as sarcasm, which was safer for her. Doing things on her own had been all she'd ever known. Depending on anyone else was never a good idea. Being let down hurt way worse than being alone.

"Then if you know how I am, why do you continue to argue?" she asked, raising her voice. "I bought this house with every intention of working on it myself. I want to do the labor so I can be proud and prove that I can do something. I'm talented when it comes to this, Ryan. Why do you keep trying to intervene and take control?"

Ryan's shaded eyes leveled hers. "I just want to make your life easier, Red. That's all. I'm not trying to take over or to run your life. I only want to see you happy."

"I'm happy when we don't argue about ridiculous things." Piper stepped back, shoved her gloves into her back pocket, jerked her ponytail holder out and smoothed all her hair back once again and secured the band.

"Listen, I'm sorry I yelled," she told him on a sigh. "I'm tired, sweaty and stressed. I shouldn't take it out on you."

"Then let me finish the roof for you or call someone who will."

"No." She shook her head. When would he get it through that thick skull of his? "I've got it."

"Stubborn as ever."

"Said the pot to the kettle," she murmured.

Piper turned and started up the ladder again. "If you're not here to help and you just came to throw insults, then go. I have work to do."

She didn't look down and didn't even glance back when she heard him bring his engine to life and pull out of her drive.

Yeah, even though they were best friends, they argued like an old married couple.

Piper laughed at the image. No way in hell would she ever marry a cowboy.

Besides, didn't he know she'd never take help unless it was an emergency? She could handle this on her own just fine, thank you very much, and if she chipped a nail doing it, well, she'd carry on and not worry about it.

Piper picked up her crowbar and got back to work. Frustration and anger was the perfect combo to put into demolishing old shingles. Because it was either concentrate on renovations or think of how sexy Ryan had looked all angry and dominant.

She didn't want to find that Neanderthal attitude of his appealing but she couldn't help it. Ryan truly cared for her, and she believed he wanted to see her happy, but she also knew he was developing feelings for her. If she kept letting him sink into every corner of her life, soon he'd want more and then what? Would they move in together? Marry?

Piper cursed when the crowbar went sliding because she wasn't concentrating. She reached out, careful of her balance, and caught the tool.

Ryan and any hormones either of them had flaring up needed to go to the back of her mind. She had to concentrate on one thing at a time.

Ryan walked around the perimeter of his recently installed fence where he hoped to train eager riders with his new horses. The men he'd hired to put the fence in had done a remarkable, efficient job.

Tugging on a few posts, Ryan was more than satisfied at the work. He'd paid a hefty sum for a speedy project and he wasn't disappointed.

Dirt and dust kicked up over his worn boots. Ryan propped a foot upon the bottom rung of the gate and looped his arms over the top as he looked out onto the fields. He couldn't wait to get Grant's Rodeo School kicked off in the spring.

Ryan was working with a man he'd met on the circuit who did some PR for events. Soon they'd have brochures and flyers to pass around to surrounding towns and mass mailings to send to various rodeo organizations.

The late fall sun beat down on him and Ryan adjusted his Stetson to shield his eyes. This new chapter of his life was both exciting and a little nerve-racking.

He was ready to settle down and start on another stage of his career and personal life, but he wasn't sure where to go beyond this school. At least, he hadn't been sure when he'd first come back, but now he was starting to see a clearer picture. He knew he'd wanted to have a more stable, calm life. Joining the Texas Cattleman's Club and teaching kids to ride was a great start, but Ryan knew as amazing as both those things were, he wanted more. Call him greedy, but he didn't care.

Piper had been the one constant in his life all these years. She'd been his best friend, his therapist, his inside-joke person at parties. They shared a bond on an intimate level that most couples never even tapped into.

He hadn't been joking or messing around when he'd discussed kissing her. The pull between them was stronger than anything he'd ever imagined. Ryan wanted to explore this newfound chemistry. Piper may be scared—oh hell, he knew she was even if she wouldn't admit it—but he wouldn't let anything happen to their friendship.

Yes, he was a guy and he was attracted to her in a "more than friends" way, but he wouldn't let their relationship fall apart over one roll in the sack. Yeah, he definitely wanted more.

Ryan stepped away from the gate and started back toward his house. He wondered if she'd like to help him with his school. She more than knew her way around horses and the rodeo. And she'd be a hell of a lot prettier sight than any other cowboy he'd hire.

Stepping through his back door, Ryan hung his black hat on the wooden peg. Crossing to the center island, he grabbed his phone and checked it for messages. One missed call from Piper, but no voice mail.

After their little argument yesterday, he wondered if she was calling to apologize for being so pigheaded. More than likely she wasn't. Knowing her, she was calling to hear *him* apologize.

Ryan tried her cell only to get her voice mail. Without leaving a message, he hung up and slid the phone into his pocket. She was at work, so maybe she didn't have time to answer or she had it turned off.

She usually took a lunch break about halfway through her shift. Ryan glanced at the clock and figured if he booked it through town, he could surprise her. She needed more surprises in her life. She needed a man to step up and be a man. She needed to see herself as a woman and not just as one of the guys.

When Ryan pulled into the lot where the paramedics usually parked, he didn't see Piper's truck anywhere, but he went inside anyway only to be told she'd taken a personal day off.

Heading back out to his truck, Ryan was really confused. Piper never took a day off work. Ever. The woman would crawl on her hands and knees to go to work to help save lives and make people comfortable.

He tried her cell again, but still no answer. Worry settled deep, especially with the whole Alex kidnapping still unsolved—at least Ryan assumed something illegal had transpired, cspccially since the state police investigator had been called in.

Ryan drove straight to her house where her shiny black truck was parked on the brick drive beside her little bungalow.

Ryan took the porch steps two at a time, rang her doorbell and opened her screen door himself when she didn't answer soon enough to suit him. The main door was locked so he used the key on his ring. Yeah, they were that good of friends. When he'd moved back permanently she'd given him a key.

Worried at the sight he'd enter into, he moved cautiously. When he rounded the corner to the living room, he found Piper on the couch, stretched out and asleep… wearing the exact same thing as yesterday.

He moved closer, surprised for so many reasons. Piper never napped, never called off work and never wore the same clothes two days in a row.

Then he saw a cord sticking out from under her back and bent to inspect. Heating pad.

A bubble of fury started within him, but he suppressed it until he knew what exactly had happened. Other than the obvious that she'd been hurt, he decided to keep his mouth shut until he had more information.

"Hey, Red," he said softly, tapping on her shoulder. "You're sleeping the day away."

She moaned, wincing as she tried to move. Her eyes opened and blinked several times as she tried to focus on him.

"Went by your work. They told me you took a personal day."

Her hand went to her head and she nodded. "I did."

"Care to tell me what happened?"

"Actually, I'd rather not," she said around a yawn. "I'm not in the mood to hear 'I told you so.'"

Ryan rested his hands on his hips. He could approach this one of two ways: he could be that sarcastic, snarky friend she probably expected or he could show some compassion and help her with whatever it was she needed. Being still a little sore from his accident, he understood her grouchy mood and not wanting to be chatty.

He eased down onto the coffee table and grabbed her hand. "I have officially deleted 'I told you so' from my vocabulary. Tell me what happened and where you're hurt."

Piper rested the back of her hand across her forehead and stared up at him. "I swear, if you say one word, I'll take my tool belt and use each and every one of those tools on you in a very unpleasant way."

"You're stalling, so it must be pretty bad."

Staring up at the ceiling, she sighed and closed her eyes. "This stupid house is only thirteen hundred square feet. I know exactly what I want it to look like and I know what to do to get it there. But when I have stupid screw-ups like this, I can't freakin' finish the project if I'm hurting myself."

"Red…"

Her eyes met his. "Right after you were here yesterday I fell off the roof."

"Damn it, Piper." Fury bubbled within him. "And you're just now telling me?"

"Actually, I called. I didn't leave a voice mail because I assumed you'd just see my number. But I'm fine." She turned her face to look at him and even offered a slight smile. "I'm a professional, remember?"

She started to sit up, winced and held on to his hand, a true sign she was hurt. But he didn't say a word. No need in saying "told you so" when she knew perfectly well he'd been right.

But he'd take being wrong any day over seeing his friend hurt. And he wasn't going anywhere until she was better. Best not to mention that to Little Miss Independent.

"Do you need to be seen?" he asked.

"No, no," she assured him as she shook her head. "Nothing some heat and rest and Motrin won't help. It's just a nuisance."

"What can I do?"

"Nothing. I was just calling earlier to tell you, but I didn't want you to worry."

Since she'd sat up, they were nearly nose to nose as he leaned in toward her. "Not worry? You fell off your roof,

Piper. You're obviously in a lot of pain and you don't want me to worry?"

"I fell off the lower part that's just over the porch," she told him, rolling her eyes. "I wasn't up on the main part."

"Don't downplay it. You didn't fall off a curb, damn it." He ran his gaze over her arms, which had a few bruises and scrapes; apparently the landscaping and bushes had caught her fall. "Take off your shirt."

Piper jerked her head back, pulled her brows together and said, "You've got to be kidding me. You go from attempting to kiss me the other night to wanting me naked? If you think I'm that vulnerable because I'm down—"

"Shut up and take your shirt off so I can see how badly you're hurt," he said, raising his voice over hers. "Can you just do one thing I say for once? Let me take these next few minutes and make sure you're okay."

"I told you I was."

Damn insufferable woman. Couldn't she just let her tough exterior down for a few minutes?

"Then humor me and let me see for myself." He purposely softened his tone because Piper was a sucker for gentlemen. It was when he yelled that she felt challenged and got her back all up. "You can barely sit up on your own, so I know it's more than a little discomfort."

She hesitated, still holding his gaze and Ryan refused to back down. Not this time. She needed to see that he was dead serious about taking care of her.

"Would it make you feel better if I took my shirt off?"

Piper rolled her eyes, but made no move to remove anything. Why did he find her stubbornness and independence so damn attractive?

"You can either take it off so I can see, or I'll do it for you." He offered her his sweetest smile. "I assure you, I won't be gentle."

Her eyes widened as her hands went to the hem. Slowly, agonizingly so, pale skin was revealed until her torso was covered in nothing but a silky lace yellow bra. Damn, how could he have forgotten about that lingerie fetish she seemed to have?

He'd seen the woman in a bathing suit for crying out loud and he was her best friend. But there was something about Piper being half naked and vulnerable that brought out the caveman in him. He wanted to pick her up, take her to bed and spend the next several days examining her injuries, making them feel better.

Ryan's gaze remained on hers as he reached out to slide his hands over the dark purple knot and bruise over her side. Goose bumps instantly dotted her skin and Ryan practically felt the tingle all through his own body.

Damn, maybe this had been a bad idea.

Too late now.

Way, way too late.

Seven

Piper closed her eyes. She wasn't used to being on the receiving end of such treatment. And the way Ryan's fingertips were gliding along her rib cage had her fighting hard to maintain her composure, to remain in her seat and not throw her arms around his neck and let him claim that kiss he'd tried for the other day.

Apparently injuries made them both horny because she was having instant flashbacks to raking her hands over his torso and the heat that had met her gaze.

"Ryan," she whispered, opening her eyes to find his face even closer than she'd first thought. "I—I'm fine."

His eyes traveled from her face to where his hand was sliding just below her breast. Suddenly the pain wasn't her first thought.

"I need to see your back, too."

She lifted her knee onto the couch and twisted her body. Ryan's gentle touch along her bare back was just as potent as when he'd been examining her front. Those fingertips may be on the surface, but she felt that contact all the way to her heart.

"How bad does it look back there?" she asked, thankful her voice didn't crack.

"Looks like you fell off a roof." His hands continued to slide softly over her skin. "You have one hell of a knot and bruise. Are you sure you don't feel like anything is broken? Shouldn't you have an X-ray just to double check?"

Piper eased back around and smiled. "I'm pretty sure I'd know if something were broken. I hurt, but not that bad. And today is the second day, so it's sorer."

His eyes held hers and Piper wanted to lick her lips, she wanted to smooth her couch-messed hair away from her face, but she did neither. She sat there, waiting on Ryan to say something, to do something.

She didn't wait long. His strong hand came up and cupped the side of her face and she couldn't help but lean into his touch, his strength.

"I can't keep denying this between us," he whispered.

Her mouth opened, anticipating his touch, his kiss.

Ryan inched closer, his mouth a breath from hers. "This is insane."

"Yes," she agreed.

"I'm going crazy wondering what you taste like."

Now Piper did lick her lips because she wanted this kiss more than she realized...or at least more than she'd been admitting to herself.

"What if this is a mistake?" she whispered, hating that her fears had been spoken aloud.

"We've made mistakes before. I prefer to take the risk so I can learn from mistakes," he told her. "But I have a feeling this risk will have a huge payoff."

He didn't wait for her to find another reason to stop. Ryan knew what he wanted and he'd waited long enough... nearly twenty years in fact.

His hands slid over her smooth cheeks as his fingertips slid into her curls and, before she could finish her gasp, his mouth was on hers.

And thank God he was sitting because to have this

woman in his arms in an intimate way after all this time made his knees weak. Warmth spread throughout his body as he coaxed her lips apart with his tongue. His hat flipped off his head and onto the floor.

She was on the same page because she met him thrust for thrust and her arms wrapped around his neck as she scooted closer.

Ryan slowly slid his lips over hers, wanting to memorize every single part of them, wanting to know exactly how she tasted and how soft she was. He wanted to know what turned her on, what buttons to push to drive her crazy.

He knew her as a friend, but he wanted to know her as a lover.

Careful of her hurt side, Ryan eased his hand down the other side of her torso, dipping in at her delicate waist and then back up to the lacy edge of her bra.

"You shouldn't be this sexy to me," he murmured against her mouth. "I shouldn't want you the way I do. God help me, I have no willpower with you."

Piper's head tipped back, exposing that long, slender neck. He took full advantage and kissed his way down, continuing a path until he reached the top of one breast.

He paused because he was pretty damn sure he'd go all the way, but he didn't want to scare her or to make her regret anything later.

His thumb stroked just at the bottom edge of her bra, slowly slipping between the wire and her breast. And that little tease of skin against the tip of his thumb made his zipper even tighter than it was before.

"This…this shouldn't go any further," she told him, breathless.

Ryan didn't remove his hands, didn't back up, but he did nod. "My mind knows that, but other parts of me think it hasn't gone near far enough."

A slow smile spread across Piper's swollen, wet lips. "I'm still reeling from the fact that my best friend wants me and is one hell of a kisser. Can we just stop right there for now?"

He leaned in, captured her lips for another brief kiss and sat back. "If you think I'm a hell of a kisser, that leaves me hope you'll want more. I'm good with leaving you wanting me."

She laughed and playfully shoved at his chest. "You're hopeless."

"I was thinking horny, but hopeless works, too."

With one last sultry glance, Piper reached for her shirt and struggled to put it back on. Ryan took the garment from her hands and slid it over her head, careful when she had to lift her arms.

"What can I do to help?" he asked. "Other than take your mind off the pain with incredible bouts of hot, sweaty sex?"

Easing back down onto the heating pad, Piper offered a smile. "Tempting as your poetic words are, this body cannot handle too much of an aerobic workout tonight."

Ryan came to his feet and propped his hands on his hips. "Okay, then. Point me in the direction of the next project that needs attention. I'm here, might as well do something."

"Other than the roof, I need to yank out those kitchen cabinets. I ordered new ones, but they're on back-order, so I do have a little time."

"Did you get that dark mahogany finish you fell in love with?" he asked.

Her eyes closed as she sighed and settled farther into the couch. "No. They were way out of my price range. I ended up getting a dark wood finish, but they are a cheaper model and brand."

Ryan glanced down at his fierce little warrior. The woman truly believed she could do all and be all. Why didn't she ever ask him for help? Just once he'd like to be the one to come to her aid without begging her to let him.

"You know I would've been more than happy to get those new cabinets for you."

Her lids flew open and green eyes met his. "You're not buying my cabinets, Ryan. That's ridiculous. You have a school you're paying through the nose to get started and you just bought a massive home. Besides, this is my little house and I love it. I'll love it with cheaper cabinets just as much as if I'd had the expensive ones. They all hold dishes and food the same way."

He knew she wasn't some pampered diva who wanted the best of everything, but he'd seen her face when they'd been looking through the sample catalog she'd brought home from the store. He'd seen how she'd froze the second she turned on to that page, how she'd stroked the picture with her fingertips.

Most women went that crazy over diamonds or fancy clothes, but his Piper was just as happy wearing her flannel, with some killer lingerie beneath. She didn't ask for the best in everything and she'd already cut enough corners with this renovating project. Now she was sacrificing something that she truly wanted because she was practical and hadn't been able to justify that extra expense.

"So the roof and the cabinets are the pressing matters?" he asked.

"I know you want to do something while you're here, but don't. Seriously." She held his gaze, pleading with him. "I'll get back at it tomorrow."

Like hell she would. But his mama raised a gentleman before she'd passed unexpectedly, so he was going to keep his mouth shut.

"I'm just curious," he told her, holding his hands up in defense. "I wouldn't dare try to overtake your project. Besides, my own ribs are still sore. Just thought if you had something small to do."

He'd not let on that he wasn't too sore that he couldn't put a dent in her kitchen or her roof. Either job would be fine for him to start tackling, but if he started now, then she'd get up and insist on helping and then she really would end up hurt.

A slight smirk flirted around that mouth he'd just sampled. "What do you say we have some lunch and not discuss all these renovations that still need to be done?"

"Tell me what you want to eat and I'll bring it to you."

"I can get up." Piper sat up and shook her head. "That pain pill is kicking in. Besides, the more I move, the more it will work the soreness out. There's only so long I can lie on that heating pad. I've probably lost five pounds in sweat since last night."

Ryan's eyes ventured to her chest, then back up. "At least you didn't lose it in the places that matter."

Piper came to her feet and smacked his chest. "You're such a pervert."

"Honest," he corrected. "I'm simply honest."

Piper sat in one of the chairs of her mismatched set in the kitchen. Ryan was prying off the countertops and setting them out the back door…much to her protesting.

"I wish you wouldn't go to so much trouble, Ryan."

He put the final piece out the door and came back in, wiping sweat off his forehead. "If I thought it was trouble, I wouldn't be doing it. And even though you griped and complained, I still want to help. I couldn't just go home and leave you here in pain. Besides, if I'm here making sure you don't overdo it, I might as well get some work done. The sooner this kitchen is back together, the sooner you can make real meals again. I'm selfish."

They'd enjoyed simple ham sandwiches and chips for lunch considering her stove was unhooked and the dishwasher wasn't installed due to the new cabinets coming soon.

And he'd sweetly convinced her that he could start the demolition of the old cabinets and if he began hurting he'd sit down. Weren't they a pair? Both stubborn, both hurt… But she'd butted heads with him long enough. She knew he truly wanted to help so she'd allowed him this small victory.

"I knew you had an ulterior motive," she told him.

Crossing the kitchen, Ryan opened the fridge and reached in to pull out a beer as he had done so many times before. Piper liked how comfortable he felt in her home. She'd never had another man in her house with whom she felt this comfortable. Ryan had always just been part of her life; she truly wouldn't know what to do without him.

He leaned against the cabinet and took a long, hard pull from the bottle. Piper admired the view of her best friend without his shirt, how his muscles flexed without any effort from Ryan. The man simply had to shift and those muscles put on quite a show.

When he licked his lips after his drink, Piper swallowed and tried to ignore that she had been taken off guard earlier with how toe-curling that kiss had been. She knew her best friend could kiss, because she'd heard talk from some ladies, but she'd never, ever, thought he'd kiss her in that way or that she'd be nearly on her knees because of the intensity of it.

"Want to bring it out in the open or just let it keep replaying in your mind?"

Piper's eyes met his and, damn him, he was grinning because he knew what had been running through her mind.

"How do you always know what I'm thinking?" she asked.

He shrugged, took another drink and sighed. "Call it a gift. I just know you better than you know yourself."

Piper rolled her eyes. "All right, Mr. Smarty Pants. What was I thinking?"

"You were thinking how you wished you would've ravished my body earlier instead of calling it quits."

Piper laughed. "Not hardly. Try again."

"Oh, you're right, that's what I was thinking." He set his beer on the top of the fridge and crossed over to her, bending and blocking her meager breeze from the fan. "You were thinking that the kiss we shared was more than you expected. You're wondering if we're going to do it again or if you should press your luck. Maybe it won't be as great the second time."

He took her hands in his, pulling her to her feet. Their faces were mere inches apart and Piper did her best to keep her breathing steady though her heart was beating rapidly.

"You're afraid to admit to yourself that you enjoyed it and you wonder what would've happened if we hadn't stopped."

Piper's eyes held his. "I'm pretty sure I know what would've happened."

"Doesn't matter that it didn't," he whispered. "One day it will."

Gone was the gentleness from earlier. Ryan gripped her arms, tipped her toward his chest until she landed against him, and then he claimed her lips.

Being trapped against such a strong, hard chest was no hardship and being in Ryan's arms somehow felt…

perfectly right. Every part of their bodies lined up where it should, making that image of the two of them in bed even more believable and real.

Just the thought of where he promised they'd end up sent a shiver down her spine. One part of her wanted to explore beyond these kisses, but the other part worried the door to friendship would slam and they'd never get back this bond they shared.

But right now, with his hands holding her firmly in place, his erection pressing into her belly and his mouth making love to hers, she almost didn't care about crossing into unchartered territory with Ryan. She almost didn't care that he was her best friend and the closest thing to family she had.

Then she remembered he was a rodeo man. A true cowboy. He had the itch in him to chase adventure and go from one arena filled with screaming fans and danger to the next.

Just like her father.

And while these kisses were totally off the charts and had her fantasy life shifting into overdrive, she knew she could never fall in love with a cowboy. There was no way she could live the life her mother had tried to put up with. And there was no way Piper could tame a cowboy.

Once that thrill of adventure entered their blood, it never left. Could Ryan really and truly be done? He was opening a school, so Piper knew he was serious about staking roots here for the long haul. But what if he grew bored? What if he needed that adrenaline rush that only the rodeo could provide?

For right now, Piper slid her arms around his waist and allowed his kiss to take her to another place. A place where they were just two people acting on this new attraction... not two people destined for heartache.

Because as scared as she was that he may decide to leave again, she couldn't deny the fact she was getting in deeper with her best friend.

Eight

"You don't have to stay, you know."

Piper pushed off the wooden porch with her bare toe and put the swing into motion. Ryan lounged across her chaise on the other side of her porch.

"I know," he told her, tipping up his cowboy hat to look at her. "I want to. Nothing else to do."

Piper laughed. "You always make me feel so appreciated. I'm so glad I rank just above nothing else to do."

"You know you also rank above castrating cattle, so don't act like you're at the bottom of my priority list."

Taking a small throw pillow from her wicker swing, Piper launched it across the porch, hitting him in the chest. The swift move made her back ache, but it was worth it.

"You've got such a smart mouth." She laughed.

"You wouldn't have me any other way," he murmured.

Still smiling, she eased back onto the swing and enjoyed the soft evening breeze. "No, I wouldn't."

For a moment Piper let the tranquility of the evening wash over her. The crickets chirping in the distance, the starry night, the warm breeze blowing across her porch. She loved having a swing out here to just sit in and reflect at the end of the day.

True, her home might still be in disrepair, but it was coming along and she was going to be able to be proud of herself when all was said and done. And the A/C was going in tomorrow afternoon. Thank you, God. Because if she had to keep seeing Ryan strip out of his shirt, mop his forehead with the garment and have his pecs flex beneath beads of sweat, she may very well die from want and lust.

"Do you remember when we'd ride our bikes past here?" Ryan asked, breaking the silence.

Piper glanced out to the sidewalk that stretched between the road and her yard. She could practically see the younger versions of the two of them peddling by. His bike had been blue and black and hers had been red with a horn. She'd loved riding up behind him and squeaking that loud thing. He'd jump every time. The trick never got old.

"I do remember," she said with a smile. "I believe I told you one day this house would be mine."

"Even back then you saw the potential in this place. I never knew why you loved it so much."

Piper shrugged, toeing off the porch again. "I always thought it looked cozy, homey. I wanted a house that I could feel loved in and this one always had toys in the yard and a mom or dad swinging up here. It just seemed like the life I wanted."

"And now?" Ryan asked. "What life are you looking for now?"

Across the porch, her eyes met his. "I wouldn't mind that life now. Though with my crazy work schedule and my time off spent here, I'm not sure the dating scene is going to happen for me for a while."

"You work too hard."

"That's because some of us aren't high and mighty celebrities making money from the rodeo circuit."

Ryan tossed the pillow back at her. "I'm not a celebrity, Red. I'm just a man who's opening a school on my ranch. I'm ready for the simple life."

Piper hugged the pillow to her chest. "You may be ready for the simple life, but I know you. You're laid-back and easygoing, but you have that reckless, adventurous streak in you from your rodeo days. If they called and asked you to come back, don't act like you wouldn't jump at the chance."

"I want a life like my parents had." His words instantly took her back to their childhood. "I want the love they shared before her death, before my father let guilt eat him alive. I know love exists. I saw it firsthand and it would've lasted forever."

Piper swallowed the lump in her throat. Ryan's mother had been killed in a car accident when his father had been driving. Piper had never seen a more distraught, broken man in all her life. The guilt, the depression, all had taken a toll on him and he'd ended up dying of a massive heart attack when Ryan was a senior in high school.

Piper knew that was another reason Ryan had been so hell-bent on getting out of town. He was running from the painful memories. And he'd buried himself in the circuit until that was all he knew, all he lived for.

"Are you sure you're not getting the itch to travel again?" she asked. "You've been home six months. That's a record for you. What about when the holidays are over? Will you be bored?"

Ryan shook his head. "I'm too busy here to be bored. I've retired for good."

Yeah, her father had, too. Twice. And all these years later that scar tissue on her heart was still deep.

"I'm not him, Piper."

She glanced up as Ryan shifted to sit on the edge of the chaise. "Whatever you think the similarities are between me and your father, my loyalty to you isn't one of them."

"It's just hard to get past how similar you two are."

Ryan came to his feet, rested his hands on his hips and stared out at the full moon that lit up the night. "You know I've never left you. Ever. I've never deserted you when you needed it. And I never intend to."

Piper sighed. "I know. I'm sorry. I'm just in a mood today. Between this house and my back being sore, I'm just a mess."

He glanced over his shoulder, throwing her one of his sexiest smiles and, like every other woman on the receiving end of that seductive grin, her insides quivered and she couldn't help but smile back.

"You're not a mess. You're allowed to be bitter about your father."

"True, but I shouldn't take it out on you." Piper slowed the swing and came to her feet, crossing to stand beside Ryan. She slid an arm around his waist and leaned against his strength. "I know there's nothing about the two of you that's comparable. You're loyal, honest and dependable."

Ryan's soft chuckle vibrated against her, so not helping her current state of battling just how sexy her best friend was and how her growing attraction was scaring the hell out of her.

"You've described the perfect dog," he replied, wrapping his arm around her shoulder.

"You know what I mean." She swatted his rock-hard stomach. "You're the one person I can always depend on. What we have is much stronger than family or most marriages, even."

"Which is why we are a perfect fit."

"Are you back to sex again?"

Ryan turned her toward him and grinned. "I'm a guy. Everything is about sex."

Piper laughed. "Well, I'm not sure if you've noticed, but not too many guys do the whole sex chat around me."

Ryan's arms cupped her shoulders through her flannel shirt. "That's their loss. I not only know what you wear beneath this heavy shirt, I also know what's inside you. Any man who doesn't appreciate what you have is a complete fool."

Piper studied his face. Nothing about those heavy-lidded eyes or that perfectly shaped mouth indicated he was teasing or joking.

"Then I must've dated fools," she murmured. "And how did we get on the topic of my sex life?"

Ryan brushed her lips with his. "Because I want to be part of it."

Piper gasped as Ryan turned that nipping playfulness into full-fledged attack. His hands slid down to her denim-covered rear and pulled her against him. Mercy, he was already aroused.

He started walking back toward the chaise. Piper had no choice but to follow. Well, she had a choice. She could either follow him or break this amazing kiss that had her lighting up on the inside. There was no way in hell she was going to stop this staggering assault on her senses.

Without breaking the kiss, Ryan eased onto the chaise, bringing Piper down to straddle his lap. His hands slid to her waist, holding her steady as she adjusted to the new arrangement.

The intimacy of this pose was not lost on her. She could feel him between her thighs as his hard torso pressed against her. His mouth continued claiming hers as his hands moved up her back, beneath her flannel.

She was so glad she'd grabbed a shower after he'd stopped by. She may not have fixed her hair nor done anything above and beyond, but she was out of yesterday's clothes and she was clean.

"Ryan," she panted against his mouth, "what are we doing?"

"Making out." He kissed along her jaw, down her throat and moved his hands from beneath her shirt to start working on her buttons. "Don't worry, I won't let this get out of control."

Piper would've laughed, but his talented hands were moving inside her shirt to her aching breasts. Out of control? They'd both let this get out of control the moment they made the conscious decision to kiss and stroke each other.

And making out at nearly the age of thirty sounded so…pathetic. Surely there was another word that didn't sound so juvenile.

But even if they'd gotten out of control, she didn't care because her body had taken over and she had no clue what rational thought was anymore.

There was no way in hell they could turn back now, but this intimacy between them was moving faster than she was comfortable with. Even though they'd been dancing around this topic for days, she still saw him as her best friend and she wouldn't give up that friendship for a quick roll in the sack.

His tongue traced the edge of her bra. Okay, so she was quite comfortable with that and maybe their trip in the sack wouldn't be so quick. The man certainly was taking his time in driving her insane with desire.

Piper arched her back because, well…she still had no control over her body when Ryan's hands and mouth were on it. And there wasn't a woman alive who could blame her. He was her best friend, he'd never deliberately hurt her and he was hot, hot, hot with a capital H-O-T.

His mouth remained on her breast as he continued to undo the rest of her buttons. When he slid the material aside, he circled his hands around her waist.

Those rough, callused palms gliding against her smooth skin provided that extra bit of friction she needed, craved. God, what would it feel like to have those hands all over her?

Piper gripped his shoulders and pressed her knees against his thighs as he moved one hand to cup her breast and then raked his tongue over her nipple.

"Ryan," she whispered, "we're on my porch."

He lifted his head and grinned. "I know."

She wasn't into PDAs, and this went way beyond that, but she didn't have any neighbors too close and shrubbery around her porch was shielding them.

Added to that, if they had to stop to go inside, she'd die. This felt too good, too right.

When his hand moved to the button of her jeans, Piper froze. "Ryan?"

"Shh. It's okay. I know you're not ready, but I want you to feel. I want you to see how right this is." He unfastened her pants, slid the zipper down and whispered, "Trust me."

She'd trusted him her whole life and now was no different.

"Lift up a tad."

Piper rose onto her knees, but dropped her forehead to his as she watched his tanned fingers slip inside her panties. She held her breath, waiting for that moment when he'd fully feel her and she him.

"Don't tense on me now, Red."

Piper closed her eyes as he parted her, sliding one finger, then two between her folds and slowly working back and forth. Before she knew it, her hips were moving, her heart was racing.

"You look beautiful," he whispered.

Her eyes locked on to his as he kept that slow, steady rhythm against her core. She tilted her hips faster, needing more and not sure how to ask for it. This wasn't weird and she didn't want to start begging and make the moment awkward.

"No hurry here," he told her. "I could touch you, watch you, all night."

"Ryan...I..."

"I know."

He cupped the back of her neck and captured her lips as his fingers moved over her, then finally in her. Between his mouth and his hand, the assault on her body was too much and the inner fight came to an end. No more trying to hold out because she was worried about their friendship. Nothing could stop her from taking this moment he was so freely giving.

Piper moaned into his mouth as her body spiraled out of control. Bursts of light flashed behind her lids; her entire body vibrated and shook as the climax slammed into her.

Ryan continued to stroke her even when her tremors ceased. Piper didn't know what to do now, but she knew there was no doubt they were headed toward sleeping together.

And she was starting to wonder why it had taken her so long to see this may not be such a bad idea.

Nine

Piper wiped at her damp cheeks, cursing herself as she turned into her drive. After all these years as a paramedic, she really should be used to seeing death. But no matter how many times patients died en route to the hospital, Piper took each death personally.

There were always the what-if and if-only moments. The question of what if she'd arrived sooner... If only those cars had pulled aside when they'd seen the ambulance coming through instead of waiting until the last minute, in turn slowing them down... Timing was crucial during a call and today's patient had not had time on his side. Piper knew no matter how fast they might have arrived, more than likely she wouldn't have been able to save his life. But she was only human and guilt consumed her with every death.

Especially today's patient. A young father who had been complaining of chest pains while running and suddenly collapsed. The look of horror on the wife's face as she'd clutched their baby to her chest would haunt Piper for a long, long time.

Life wasn't fair and Piper was damn sick of bad things happening around her. Alex still hadn't regained his memory, but he'd been out of the hospital for a few days. Hopefully being back home on his own turf would trigger something.

Cara was nearly attached to his side and Piper knew the woman was barely holding it together, clinging to a thin thread of hope that the old Alex would soon emerge and they could go back to the happy couple they once were.

The front of Ryan's truck stuck out from the back of her house. What on earth was he doing parked on the grass behind her house?

Piper pulled right up in front of the garage and grabbed her purse. As she walked around the side of the house, her back door was propped wide open and Ryan's signature heavy-metal music was blaring out into the yard. He obviously had a warped mind if he considered that yelling music.

But she had her favorite bands and he had his. Heavy metal was by far his favorite type of music and Pantera was his all-time favorite band.

Music was one area they definitely did not agree on, but if that was the man's only flaw, well then, she had a true winner on her hands. Good thing she didn't have too-close neighbors.

She stepped into her kitchen and her purse dropped to the floor with a thud. Ryan jerked around, smiled and reached over to turn down his radio.

"You're home earlier than I thought," he told her, resting his hands on his narrow hips. "I was hoping to be finished here."

Piper didn't know what she wanted to stare at more: Ryan with his shirt off, sweat glistening in each and every dip and crevice around his pecs and abs, or the brand-new cabinets he'd installed.

And not just any cabinets, but the ones she'd wanted originally. The crazy-expensive ones she'd denied herself because they were way out of her budget.

As if her emotions needed another hit today. Piper's

tear button was pressed again and she cupped her mouth to keep from making a total fool of herself. Her damn quivering chin was a dead giveaway and she was such an ugly crier with a red, snotty nose, puffy eyes and blotchy skin. Yeah, she certainly wasn't turning any heads with that frightening look.

"Red, it's just cabinets." Ryan crossed the room and took hold of her shoulders, forcing her to look at him. "I didn't mean to make you cry. I thought you'd be excited."

Piper shook her head, taking in a deep breath. "I can't believe you did this, Ryan. It's…it's… Why did you change the order?"

He shrugged. "Because this is what you wanted."

Damn it, she wanted to be upset with him, but how could she when his sole reason for doing this was to make her happy? His reasoning was so simple, so selfless. And that's exactly how he'd been his whole life from the moment he'd walked up to her on the playground so she wasn't lonely or uncomfortable. Even when she'd hit him, he'd stuck around to make sure she was happy.

There wasn't a selfish bone in Ryan Grant's body. Plus, he caught her at a weak moment and she didn't even have the energy to be angry even if she wanted to.

"These were expensive," she insisted, stating the obvious.

He shrugged. "I only shelled out the difference in what you had already put down for the others. You paid for most of these, if that makes you feel any better."

Her eyes drifted over his shoulder to the new mahogany cabinets. Even without the countertop in place, they were stunning and really made her little bungalow's kitchen look classy.

"They're perfect," she told him, bringing her gaze back to meet his. "I'll never be able to thank you."

"I didn't do it for thanks. I did it because I care for you and I want to see you happy." He studied her face and frowned. "Want to tell me what had you in tears before you came home?"

Piper stepped back, wiping her face again and trying to paste on a convincing smile. "It was nothing."

Resting his hands on his narrow waist, Ryan cocked his head. "Piper, you can't lie to me, darlin'. Tell me what happened. Is it Alex?"

"No, no. I talked with Cara last night and he still hasn't regained his memory."

"Something happen at work?"

Piper turned toward the cabinet and slid her hand along the smooth door. She moved to the window above where the sink would be installed and stared out at her meager backyard.

"We lost a patient on the way to the hospital," she told him. "He was around our age. He had a wife and a new baby."

"Damn."

Piper turned around and leaned back against the edge of the cabinet. "It happened just before my shift ended and I thought I'd come home, soak in the tub and get my cry out of my system. I didn't know I'd have company."

Ryan closed the space between them, cupping her cheeks. "I'm not company, Red. If you want to get that cry out, go right ahead. My shoulders are strong. I can handle you."

Piper resisted for all of a second before Ryan just pulled her against his hard body. She wrapped her arms around his waist and rested her cheek against his warm, bare chest.

"Quit always trying to be so damn strong, Piper." He stroked her back, then reached up to pull her ponytail free. His hands slid through her hair. "I don't need you to put up a front around me, ever. Just be yourself, let it out. No one has to know you had a moment of vulnerability."

Yeah, but she would know. Unfortunately she just couldn't keep the emotions bottled up any longer. Piper let her buried sobs rise to the surface. She clutched Ryan's back, her forehead resting against the middle of his bare chest.

She inhaled his masculine scent and didn't care that he was all sweaty. She needed to draw from his strength, from his affection.

"You should've seen her face," she cried. "His wife was holding their baby, her eyes held hope, but I knew he wasn't going to make it. I couldn't even look at her, Ryan. I'm a coward. I knew he was fading and I wanted to get him into the ambulance before we lost him. I didn't want her to see that."

"You did what you could."

Piper sniffed, her body shook as more sobs tore through her. "I couldn't do a damn thing to save him. Now that baby will grow up with no father and his wife is all alone."

Ryan knew that right there was the main reason this patient had hit her so hard. Even though her father hadn't passed away, he was gone from her life and she still felt that void. Piper had never had closure, had never been able to fill the gap he had left in her heart. The only things she had to cover that hole were years of bitterness and anger.

"You can't save everyone," he told her. "You're human. Only God controls who stays and who goes."

Piper slid her hands around, flattened them against his chest and lifted her face to look at him. Ryan wiped the pads of his thumbs across her cheeks and held her face firm between his palms.

"I'm sorry I fell apart on you."

Ryan smiled, nipped at her lips. "I'm not. I like knowing you want to lean on me for comfort. I want to be here for you, Piper. For everything."

Couldn't she see that? After all these years, couldn't she see that he was ready to settle down now, that he was back for good? That he was finally ready to sow permanent roots?

"What happed to the A/C installation?" he asked, hoping to take her mind off work.

"Sorry, they had to reschedule. I'm so used to it now, I didn't think. You worked all day in this heat?"

He shrugged. "It's Texas. I can stand the heat."

Her shining eyes held his and Ryan moved in closer. Slowly, so slowly, in case she wasn't ready for his intimate touch. But he had to taste her, had to show her that she was special, that she was cherished even when she was vulnerable…especially when she was vulnerable and let that guard down.

He slid his hand across her cheek, beyond her ear and to the back of her head, pulling her in toward him.

"Stop me," he whispered, warned. "Stop me from doing this again."

"I can't."

Yeah, neither could he.

Ryan stole her lips and just like the other times he'd kissed her, a wave of perfection consumed him. Perhaps this was the woman he was meant to settle down with. Perhaps this woman who'd been in his life since childhood and through school and the wild ride on the circuit was the one who would stand by his side until he was old and gray.

Piper's arms slid around his neck as she toyed with the damp ends of his hair. Her soft moans filled him as his tongue danced with hers.

Allowing his hands to travel down her back, Ryan cupped her rear and tugged her against his hips so she could see just how she affected him. This was beyond friendship and, if he were honest with himself, they'd passed friendship well before they'd kissed the first time. They'd passed it the instant he'd moved back, considered her naked and in his bed, then imagined her never leaving his side or his new ranch.

Ryan took a handful of her shirt and tugged it from her work pants. He needed skin, her skin. That soft, delicate, satiny skin that always felt so amazing beneath his roughened hands. He wanted that goodness, that near innocence she could bring to his life. And he wanted her to see just how special she was.

Moving his hands around to her belt, he unfastened her pants when she gasped his name.

"What's wrong?" he asked.

Her eyes locked on his as she panted and licked her moist lips. "I—I…"

She closed her eyes, shaking her head, and Ryan eased back from his grasp on her disheveled clothes. Whatever she was about to say, she was right.

"We can't do this." He smoothed down her shirt and took a step back, ignoring the devil on his shoulder telling him to take what his body craved. "You're vulnerable and I'm horny. That would make for a really bad wreck in this relationship."

Piper laughed. "That's one very blunt way of putting it."

"Have you ever known me to be any other way?" he asked.

She adjusted her belt. "No, I haven't. That's why I admire and care for you so much."

Ryan watched as her shaky hands refastened her belt and he knew they needed to get out of this house, away from the temptation of being alone with their jumbled emotions.

"You up to going out tonight?" he asked.

Her head popped up and she grinned. "What did you have in mind?"

"We could go to Claire's."

Piper's smile widened and Ryan felt the kick in the stomach that had been associated with that potent action.

"I'd love to. That's exactly what I need."

"I have a few things to do over at the school first. I had some men working on a new barn today and I need to catch them before they leave. But I can be back in a few hours." He smacked a kiss on her cheek. "Try to leave the flannel and jeans in the closet. 'Kay, Red?"

Rolling her eyes, she turned to head toward her room. "Lock the door behind you, slick."

Whistling as he headed to his truck, Ryan knew that even if Piper came out for their date in her most worn plaid flannel, holey jeans and beat-up work boots, he'd still be thrilled to be seen with her at the upscale restaurant in Royal. He never did care too much what people thought. They were going to talk whether you wanted them to or not. He always figured if they were talking about him, they were leaving others alone and he had thick skin.

He was anxious to take Piper to Claire's. They hadn't been to the restaurant before together and he wanted to start staking his claim, barbaric as that may sound. He wanted Piper to get used to the idea that he was putting down roots in Royal and he intended for his life to intertwine with hers. Forever.

Ten

This was absolutely silly.

Piper stood in front of her mirror wearing only a lacy black thong and matching demi bra. Yeah, this was as pretty as her wardrobe got because nearly everything in her closet consisted of flannel or denim. She had a couple of dresses, mainly because so many people were getting married lately, but she wasn't going to wear a dressy dress to Claire's. Though the upscale restaurant's romantic ambience called for something above plaid flannel, being overly dressed just to eat dinner simply wasn't her style.

She sighed and glanced at the clock on her bedside table. Ryan would be back in about thirty minutes looking all freshly showered and sexy as hell. The man could wear anything, throw on his Stetson and look like he'd just stepped off the pages of a calendar featuring hot, hunky cowboys.

Piper went back to her closet, hoping something had changed since the last time she'd peeked in there.

Fingering plaid shirt after plaid shirt, she stared at the few dresses she owned. The bright blue was her favorite because it was simple, but it was also very striking and she really didn't want to call attention to herself.

Her eyes moved over the black one and she paused. Black was a nice "I want to blend with the crowd" color.

She yanked the sleeveless dress from the hanger before she could change her mind. While she hated dresses, she didn't want to embarrass Ryan. He was taking her out to keep her mind off of her terrible workday...and probably so they could get out of the confines of her steamy house where the sexual tension had settled into every nook and cranny.

Was he classifying this as an actual date? Was he trying to go beyond friendship and make things more intimate? So many questions, so many worries.

But for tonight, she wasn't going to analyze everything to death. No, really. She wasn't. Piper vowed to herself that she would enjoy Ryan's company and this was no different than if they were grabbing a piece of pie at the Royal Diner. This time they would just be dressed up, eating steak and using the cloth napkins at Claire's.

She slid the dress over her head and groaned when her curly hair sprang from her shoulders. Could she be any more clichéd? Curly red hair and green eyes with a fuller figure. She wasn't a supermodel-thin blond...she was just curvy and curly.

As she looked at the black dress, she started to wonder if she just looked like a witch. Yeah, this wouldn't do. Yanking it off, she tossed it onto her unmade bed and went back to the closet. She found a dress in a Kelly green that matched her eyes and prayed she wouldn't look ridiculous in it. The thing still had the tags on it because she just knew another of her friends would get married soon.

At this rate she'd have to start housing her dresses in the guest-room closet because she was accumulating so many. She wasn't much of a dress girl, but a small sliver of her enjoyed dressing up for her friends' weddings and bridal showers.

The sleeveless wrap dress looked much better, she admitted as she tied the satiny ribbons at her waist. But she refused to be one of those women who tried on every stitch of clothing in her closet and claimed she had nothing. This was Ryan; he wouldn't care what she wore.

Now for the shoes. Work boots were probably a no. Other than those and a few tennis shoes she worked out in, she had one pair of dressy sandals that had a low, very low, heel.

She slid into the silver sandals and threw on earrings before she tried to tackle her hair. That was always a losing battle. But with the elegant restaurant, she opted to pull her hair back as opposed to going in looking like she just finished her shift as a circus clown.

The good thing about the curls was they made for a cute messy bun at the nape of her neck, which she secured with a heavy silver clasp that had been her mother's. That was one piece of jewelry she would never part with and often wore even with flannel and denim. She always felt a connection with her mother.

By the time she'd applied a bare minimum of makeup and a little more gloss than usual, her front door opened and shut. Ryan's boots clicked down the hardwood in the hall.

"You still in the shower, Red?"

"Don't you wish," she called back.

When he whistled she turned from checking her purse on the bed to see him leaning against the doorway. His eyes raked down her body and took a slow, leisurely stroll back up.

"If you keep looking at me like that we won't get out of this bedroom," she joked, hoping he didn't pick up on how nervous she was all of a sudden.

"That would be fine with me," he told her. "You look

hot. Care to torture me further and tell me what you're wearing beneath that dress?"

"Black lace."

Ryan's eyes closed and he sighed. "I asked for it."

Laughing, Piper slid her purse strap over her shoulder and headed to the door. "Come on, big guy. We need to get out of here before we miss our reservations."

"I'd rather move toward the bed," he grumbled.

That made two of them, but someone had to keep their wits about them and for now it looked to be her. Though the heat in his heavy-lidded eyes made her tingle in places she'd never tingled before... So what would happen once they got into bed?

She smiled as she moved down the hall. Yes, there would be a when, not an if. She'd resigned herself to the fact she wanted to sleep with her best friend. She wanted to know him on a deeper, more intimate level, but she wasn't sure if she was ready yet.

As she reached for the knob of her front door, strong hands came up to grip her shoulders, spinning her around and pinning her against the door. Being trapped between a hard panel of wood and a hard panel of...well...

"You're not fighting fair," he murmured as his lips hovered over hers and his hands held her in place.

"I wasn't fighting at all," she chided.

His eyes darted to her mouth. "That's what makes this so bad. You're not even trying and you're driving me out of my ever-lovin' mind."

To know she had that much power over Ryan warmed her, made her feel like the vixen she never knew she could be.

"You're looking pretty sexy yourself, cowboy," she told him.

A crisp black dress shirt pulled across taut, broad shoulders. And he'd forgone the Stetson and just settled for that sexy, messy bed-head he wore so well.

"Did you get to talk to the guys about the new barn?" she asked.

Ryan's lips tipped into a grin. "Trying to distract me?"

"Just trying to stay focused so we can get to the restaurant."

"Yeah." He sighed. "We're ahead of schedule and I'm ready to start bringing in more livestock."

A lock of dark hair fell over one bright blue eye. Piper slid her fingertip across his forehead to move the strand aside.

The muscle in his jaw ticked, his nostrils flared, and Piper's body tightened in response.

"Are you sure we can't stay in?" he whispered, eyes on her mouth. "I don't want to think about the school or anything else. Just you. Us. And whatever these feelings are."

The man was more tempting than Satan himself, but she had to take this slowly. Over twenty years of friendship couldn't be thrown aside for a few hours of sweaty passion. She had to think long term here.

"You make it hard to be strong for both of us, Ryan." She tried to make light of the situation, but soon…soon she would let down her guard and her own emotions would come flooding out. "Just give me some time."

"Baby, we've known each other for so long, what's a few more days?" He grinned, his eyes meeting hers. "You're worth waiting for, but that doesn't mean I can't give you, and me, something to think about."

His lips moved softly over hers, lightly at first, then he coaxed hers apart with his tongue. His mouth was firm yet tender, and Piper nearly melted against him. She knew what he was doing. Seduction at its finest and Ryan Grant was the president of the club.

Ryan leaned into her a bit more. From torso to knees they were connected with only the thin barrier of their clothing. Damn material.

Piper nearly lost her mind with want, with need, but Ryan pulled back and smiled, the same smile he used to throw at cameras when he was asked about the circuit. There was love in that smile and Piper was going to have to think about what that meant.

"You ready? I'm starving," he told her. "I hope you can keep your hands off me tonight."

Piper smacked his chest and turned the doorknob behind her back. "I'll try to resist and let you have a nice meal without me molesting you."

"I can make sacrifices anytime you feel like molesting me, Red. You just say the word. Hell, I could probably eat my steak, drink my beer and enjoy your molesting all at the same time. I'm good at multitasking."

The warm evening air greeted them as they stepped onto her narrow porch. "That's such a guy answer."

"Babe, I'm all guy. And when you're ready to find that out firsthand, you let me know."

He moved by her, opening the door of his full-size black truck.

When she gripped the armrest on the door and put her foot on the running board, Ryan cupped his hands around her rear end.

"Need a spotter?" he asked.

Piper glanced over her shoulder to see him squatting, smirking and staring up at her. "Get your hands off my butt, slick."

"Just trying to help a friend."

His hands remained until she swatted him. "You're trying to cop a feel, pal."

"I don't know what you're talking about. Simply helping you get into the truck."

Piper climbed in, by herself, and stared back at him. "I've climbed into this truck, and my own, for years. You've never offered to *spot* me before."

"A guy can't decide to just help without being ridiculed? I'm hurt."

Ryan closed the door to her laughter and Piper crossed her legs. This was going to be one very interesting "date" if he kept up this playful flirtation. She liked it.

Ryan was going to die. He couldn't handle this anymore. The romantic ambience of Claire's with its crisp white table linens topped with fresh floral centerpieces and tapered candles… Between all of that and the damn wrap dress just begging for him to peel off of Piper, he didn't know how he was going to make it through the rest of dinner.

Thank God their steaks had arrived and he was able to concentrate on the big slab of meat and not the vee of that material that crossed between her breasts.

How could he possibly even think of ordering dessert when he only wanted to taste what sat across from him?

"You're going to get us thrown out of here if you don't quit looking at me like I'm a piece of chocolate cake."

Ryan grinned. "It's a shame you're not."

"You need a new topic, cowboy. I'm well aware of where your mind stands, but can you think of something else to focus on? Your new school? Alex? Anything?"

"I suppose." Ryan shrugged. "The school is coming right along and I have some teenage boys who are helping and getting the hang of how things will be run. I'm hoping to hire them to help the younger kids and at the same time train them a bit more and get them ready for the circuit. There's one in particular that has potential."

"That's great." She beamed. "You'll be awesome at this, Ryan, I just know it. Having a rodeo school for kids is perfect for you."

Ryan loved her smile, and it warmed his heart that she was just as excited as he was about the project.

"Any more from Alex?" he asked, trying to stay off the topic of his hormones and the fact she was sex on a stick tonight.

"Cara didn't return my call earlier, so I haven't heard anything." Piper eased forward, resting her elbows on the white cloth. "I hate to bother her all the time, but I care for Alex and I worry for her. I don't want her to feel like I'm just neglecting her."

"Cara has so many friends who care for her. She's overwhelmed, but just the fact you called tells her you care. She'll be fine, Piper."

Piper smiled. "See, you went ten whole seconds without flirting or talking about sex."

"I'm trying."

"I know something that will kill your…personal issue," Piper said. "I have to go replace the emergency equipment that was destroyed in the break-in at the clubhouse's day-care center. I didn't get there the other day."

"That still pisses me off. To vandalize where children will be watched and cared for all because some insane person doesn't want women in the club? It's too late to change that, so let's just move forward and stop creating more of a mess."

"That's why you're so awesome." She smiled. "You don't agree with those who believe women have no place at the TCC. I think it's a great thing and the day-care facility is brilliant."

"Any idea what you have to replace?" Ryan asked, taking a long pull of draft beer from his pilsner glass.

"I was told there are several first-aid kits that were damaged and the CPR cart. The entire lock cabinet was shattered, too. I told them I would get everything in order so the safety inspector can come finalize the area."

Ryan watched Piper's delicate hand as she used a fingertip to circle her wineglass. Those hands had saved lives, held on to loved ones who were in fear; they'd lassoed horses and even helped bring foals into this world. His Piper was one very intriguing, diverse woman and he couldn't wait to feel those hands on his body.

"I thought that was you two over here."

Ryan turned as Piper did and saw Dave Firestone and Mia Hughes approaching their table. Dave was Alex's business rival and his beautiful fiancée, Mia, was Alex's housekeeper. A little conflict there, but they were making it work. The newly engaged couple stood hand-in-hand and Ryan was so happy that they had worked out their problems and were now headed down the aisle…like so many others in Royal lately. Engagements were becoming an epidemic.

"You look beautiful, Mia," Piper exclaimed with a wide grin across her face. "Are you two celebrating anything special other than being engaged?"

Mia patted Dave's arm. "Being engaged and the fact Alex is home. We're trying to pin down a date for the wedding right now."

"Have the police contacted you again since Alex was found?" Dave asked.

"We talked to them at the site and then I went down the other day to tell them all I knew," Piper said.

"Nathan Battle stopped by the ranch several days ago," Ryan said, mentioning his friend, the sheriff. "I just hope they catch the bastard who was behind that. Nathan was pretty thorough when he and I talked. And since he and Alex are friends and he's invested, I know he won't rest until he gets to the bottom of this mess."

Dave wrapped his arm around Mia's waist. "At least we can move forward with the wedding and not feel like someone is missing."

"Have you found a dress?" Piper asked.

Mia's smile widened. "I did and it's perfect."

"What color are your bridesmaids' dresses?"

"I'm thinking of going with a neutral so the flowers really pop, but I'm not sure."

Ryan watched as Piper's face lit up at the wedding talk. She may think she wasn't bride material, but Ryan could totally see her in a long white gown, all that fiery hair spilling down her back.

He shook the image off. Was he really and truly ready to be the man at the other end of that aisle?

"I'm really happy for you guys," Ryan told them. "Would you care to join us? We were just about to order dessert."

"Oh, no." Dave shook his head. "We've already had the chocolate cake. We're actually thinking of having them do our wedding cake, so we wanted to sample it again."

"The sacrifices he makes for this wedding," Mia joked.

"You sure you don't want to sit and visit?" Piper asked.

Dave and Mia met each other's eyes, their smiles widened.

"We really need to head home," Dave said, not taking his eyes off Mia. "But it was great to see you two out and looking so cozy. Maybe there will be another engagement soon?"

Piper's mouth fell open, but Ryan just laughed. "We wouldn't want to steal your thunder, pal."

As the happy couple walked away, Ryan glanced back to Piper who was glaring at him.

"You let them think we're here on a date," she said between gritted teeth.

"Why not? We are."

"But they don't need to know that."

Ryan reached across the table and took hold of her small hand. "Listen, you better get used to the fact I want you. Not just in bed, Piper. I want you in my life as more than just a friend. If that scares you, then join the club. I scared the hell out of myself when I finally admitted it, but I won't live my life scared. I want us to be seen together in public as a couple."

He eased forward, tugging her until she was leaning across the table, as well.

"And also get used to the fact that one day, very soon, you'll be in my bed and we won't be done after just one time."

By the time they left and were headed back to Piper's house, Ryan was beyond sexually frustrated. Seeing her curves shift beneath that dress, knowing that bow on the side was the only thing holding it in place was driving him completely mad.

But because this was his Piper, he wouldn't push it. She was a very independent woman, very strong-willed and when she wanted something, she'd come after it with everything in her. He couldn't wait to become the prey instead of the hunter.

Ryan pulled into her brick drive and killed the engine. "I'll walk you in."

Of course, by the time he got around to her door, she was already out.

"I would've gotten the door for you," he told her, taking her hand and leading her up the wide walkway.

"I'm capable of getting out of a car, Ryan."

He turned back to her, the moon casting a soft glow around her and the streetlamp highlighting one side of her delicate face.

"I know what you're capable of," he murmured, moving in closer. "I know everything about you, Red. But you need to know that this is moving into the territory of dating and I plan on doing more for you. You deserve a man who will treat you like a lady and not just as one of the guys."

"You treat me like one of the guys," she retorted.

Ryan squeezed her hands and grinned. "Trust me, I don't think of you as one of the guys. And maybe it's time I treat you better. You shouldn't always have to be seen in flannel and work boots, Piper. You're a lady and I know you wear very ladylike things beneath those work clothes. Why not showcase that a bit more?"

Piper shrugged. "I don't know any other way. I'm comfortable in my work clothes."

"Well you're a knockout now and you look comfortable." He eased in, letting his lips glide gently across hers. "You're not feeling out of your element, are you? All dressed up and on a date with me?"

Her lids fluttered closed. "No. I feel…"

"What?" he whispered. "What do you feel?"

Piper tipped her face up toward the moonlight. The column of her neck combined with the deep vee of her dress made for some very sexy skin exposure and damn if his hands didn't itch to stroke every inch and then follow through with his tongue.

So he did.

With the tips of his fingers he started between her breasts where the material met, then slid them up and over her throat and around to her jawline. Easing down, he opened his lips and followed the path until he got to her jaw, then he moved around to her waiting lips.

Piper opened for him, surprising him when she took hold of his face between her hands and stole the control right out from under him. Her body eased against his, her lips took everything he was offering. Slender hips bumped his and his pants grew even tighter. Seemed like every time he was around her lately he was hard as a horny teenager.

She groaned slightly and eased back, still framing his face in her hands.

"You make me forget that I'm supposed to be the strong one here," she said, licking her moist lips. "You make me want things that I know I shouldn't. But you make me also wonder what this would be like. Would we be better? I can't imagine anything better than what we already have."

Ryan reached up, taking her face in his hands, mirroring her actions. "I *know* we'd be better. I know it because I wouldn't allow this relationship to go anywhere else but up. I meant it when I said I was here for good, Piper. I know you're scared because of your dad—"

"Ryan—"

"No, you will listen," he told her, pulling her face closer and looking into her eyes. "I care about you on a level I didn't know possible. Don't compare me to a man who shut you out and only remembers you a couple occasions per year. I know more about you than he ever will. And I damn well care about you more than he ever did."

Piper closed her eyes. "You're so good for me, Ryan. But that fear is just part of me. I've never lived without it."

"Then maybe it's time you started." He kissed her hard then eased back. "And when you've conquered that fear, I better be the first to know."

Without another word or a backward glance, Ryan made the hardest decision to date. He marched to his truck and got the hell out of temptation's way because one more look from Piper's misty eyes and he would've gotten all soft on her.

And that would've pissed both of them off.

Eleven

Piper pulled into the TCC clubhouse parking lot and sighed. She was not looking forward to teaching the day-care workers CPR or fixing the vandalized equipment.

Her mind was still on Ryan Grant and last night's promising kiss and touching words. He was putting it all out there, laying his emotions and heart on the line. The man never knew fear, never considered failure. He'd always been that way: careless, free and courageous.

But he'd never been hurt, never had the stability of life ripped from beneath him. He'd always known what he wanted and he went after it full-force.

And apparently he had his sights set on her.

Nerves settled low in her belly as Piper started up the sidewalk toward the clubhouse. The large single-story stone building with its slate roof was very masculine, very eye-catching. Until recently it had been an all-male bastion, with membership off-limits to women and children not welcome at all.

Such a shame that now when the club was getting with the times and allowing women to join, some members found it necessary to fight overturning the archaic rule.

Piper stepped into the clubhouse and took a left toward the new child-care facility. Perhaps some of the disgruntled men were grouchy because the new day care took the place of the old billiards room. Oh, well, wasn't her job to judge, only to fix the equipment and help the staff get certified in CPR.

When she stopped in the manager's office, a petite blonde sat at the desk muttering to herself and working on what appeared to be a spreadsheet.

Piper tapped the back of her knuckles on the doorframe. "Excuse me."

The lady with a short blond bob jerked her attention toward Piper. "Oh, sorry. I was lost in thought. Can I help you?"

"I'm Piper Kindred." She stepped into the office, extended her hand. "I'm the paramedic who is supposed to replace the equipment and certify some of the day-care workers."

The woman shook her hand. "I'm Kiley Roberts, the new manager. So great to meet you."

Kiley had soft brown eyes and a kind smile. Piper could easily see her working with children and putting worried parents at ease.

"I stopped to look at the equipment the other day, but I missed you," Piper said. "Is this a good time to get into the facility? I came early since we're not scheduled to do the certification for another hour."

"This is perfect." Kiley came to her feet. "Come on back."

She punched in a security code and the locked door to the facility clicked open. "I straightened that room up after the police went through it, but I am not sure what all needs to be replaced."

Piper gripped her heavy duffel full of supplies. "I'll figure it out."

"Are you a member here, too?" Kiley asked, flipping

on the light in the small utility room where the medical equipment was stored.

Piper laughed. "No. I have too much on my plate to get involved with this he-man, she-man battle."

"Oh, I've already heard from both sides about the women and children. I'm not sure why some of the male members who voted against it feel the need to vent to me, but I listen. Most times when people complain, it's just to get their emotions off their chest and then they feel better." Kiley smiled. "But arguing and complaining about it now seems a bit silly."

Setting her black bag down, Piper unzipped it and pulled out basic first-aid kits. "It's only a matter of time before the dissenting members come around. Besides, I think the few women who are members are strong and it's only a matter of time before more come aboard."

"I agree," Kiley said, easing a hip onto the small desk in the corner. "Is there something I can help you do?"

Piper studied the damaged kits and decided to toss them all. No need in keeping items that were probably no longer sanitary.

"Actually, you can keep me company," Piper said. "Unless you'd like to get back to that spreadsheet."

"Believe me, I love my job, but spreadsheets were created by the devil."

Piper laughed. "Tell me about yourself. Do you have any kids of your own?"

"I have one." Kiley's smile widened, her eyes sparkled. "She's two and her name is Emmie."

"Two years old?" Piper asked, raising a brow. "You must have your hands full."

"I do, but in a good way. She's my world."

"Is your husband a member of TCC?"

That bright smile faltered, but Kiley recovered. "I'm

divorced and he has nothing to do with Emmie. So, no. He's not a member."

Way to go, Piper. Would you like salt and a napkin to go with that foot you just shoved in your mouth?

"Sorry," she said.

"No worries. I'm better off without him."

Piper nodded. "My parents are divorced and my mother always said the same thing. Times were hard for her—for us—but I know we were better without my father than we would've been with him."

"I won't lie, being a single mother isn't easy, but I'd do anything for Emmie. I've just never understood how anyone could walk away from a marriage, let alone a child."

Piper swallowed. She'd always wondered the same thing.

Silence settled in as Piper exchanged the first-aid kits and put the old ones in her bag to dispose of later.

"What about you?" Kiley asked after a bit. "Is your husband a member of TCC?"

"Oh, I'm not married."

Kiley shook her head. "Are we two of the select few in Royal who aren't engaged or already married? People are hooking up around here like crazy."

Piper laughed as she locked the cabinet and gathered her bag. She and Kiley stepped into the hall.

"There are a few single women left, not many though," Piper told her.

Men's voices filtered down the hall. Piper and Kiley turned toward the entryway where Josh Gordon stood chatting with another TCC member.

"That's one of the members, Josh Gordon," Piper pointed out. "I'm not sure of the other man's name. I think he's fairly new."

Piper didn't miss the way Kiley's back and shoulders instantly stiffened, her eyes focused on Josh. Interesting.

"Do you know Josh?" Piper asked.

Kiley jerked her head around. "What? Oh, no."

"He's one of the members who isn't keen on the idea of women and children on the premises."

Kiley crossed her arms over her simple white shirt. "Really? I assume he's single then if he's not interested in the equal rights."

"Yes. Also one of the few single men in Royal." Piper glanced at her watch. "I have to go grab some more things from my car for the CPR class and for the cart in the medical room. I'll be right back."

Kiley smiled. "I'll be here."

As Piper walked away, she caught Kiley's eyes going back to Josh. There was a story there. Piper didn't know what, and it wasn't any of her business, but something about Josh did not sit well with the cute new day-care manager.

Piper took her bag to her truck and pulled out another duffel with items for the CPR class. The last thing Piper needed to do was to get involved in someone else's personal issues. God knew she had enough of her own.

She knew Ryan and there was no way he was going to allow the sexual tension between them to die down. He wouldn't shy away from it the way she might try to. That man would tackle it head-on and Piper had a feeling if she didn't hang on for the ride, Ryan would bring her along anyway. His charm alone was very potent.

Two days later Piper set her purse on the newly installed granite countertop and smiled.

She shook off her damp arms. The rain beat hard against the kitchen window and she wondered where the sneaky home renovator was. She hoped he didn't think because they were growing closer that it meant he needed to go above and beyond on her home. She definitely didn't want things to start getting awkward here.

Ryan came through the doorway from the front of the house. Hands on his hips, brow furrowed, he asked, "You like?"

It had been a day from hell because she'd had to work almost four hours extra when a new hire had decided *not* to show up. Piper really hated that her emotions were all over the place from stress. Plus, when it came to Ryan, her emotions had not found solid ground and she didn't know how to feel. Damn female hormones.

"I understand why you finished the roof when I hurt myself," she started, feeling tears burn her eyes. "I even let the cabinets slide because I'm shallow and I was thrilled I had the upgraded ones. But yesterday you laid the tile for the shower and floor in my bathroom and today I see my front door was installed."

"So why is this a problem?" he asked. "Because you wanted to do it all? Piper, you've done an insane amount of work on this house. I just wanted to help you and I didn't have anything pressing to do today. The school is ahead of schedule. I worked there this morning and there's nothing I can do until the inspector comes in a couple of days anyway. Spending my spare time here keeps me busy."

Piper shoved the wayward curl off her forehead and tucked the strand behind her ear. Damn crazy hair of hers. As if she needed something else to bother her today.

"You look like you had a bad day," Ryan observed, studying her face. "Why don't you come into the bathroom and help me with that tile design behind the new vanity. After that little piece is done, that room will be finished. Would that make you feel better?"

Piper smiled, forcing herself to be happy he was so handy and understood her love of hard labor, too. "I suppose, but only if I get to control the tile cutter."

Ryan extended his hand and guided her toward the bathroom. "I wouldn't have it any other way."

Piper stepped through the doorway to her master suite bath. The blue glass tile for the open shower sparkled. He'd just begun the backsplash above the sink and she could already picture the beauty.

"I'm so glad I went with the brighter blue in here," she told him. "It's so hard to tell from those itty-bitty samples, but this is gorgeous."

Ryan's hand slid around her waist as he tugged her close. "Sometimes you need to see the whole picture, but beauty normally comes from something small and builds over time."

Piper eased back to look over her shoulder. "Are you getting deep on me, cowboy? I'm just talking about a bathroom."

"Maybe I'm talking about you." He kissed her nose, swatted her butt and stepped around her. "Now quit trying to get me out of my clothes and get to work in here."

Laughing, Piper stepped over the tile saw and moved toward the work area. "I think we both know I wouldn't have to try to get you out of your clothes. They'd just fall off if I said the word."

"Oh, what a glorious day that will be," he said with a wide grin and sigh.

The house shook as thunder boomed and the lights flickered, but came right back on.

"Time for a storm," Piper told him. "The sky was pretty black and that rain really cut loose as I was walking in the back door."

"We need the rain, but I hate storms."

Piper laughed. "I know you do. You're living in the wrong state, you know."

Ryan shrugged, picked up a small, patterned piece of uncut tile and measured it next to the wall. "I wouldn't live anywhere else. I love this town. I knew when I wanted to settle down and make a permanent home, I wouldn't go anywhere else."

"Even with all those places you traveled to?"

"Royal is still the best place on earth." He set the tile down on the counter and looked her in the eye. "Best scenery I've ever been exposed to."

"Ryan, you aren't playing fair."

A naughty grin kicked up one corner of his mouth. "I'm not playing and I never claimed to be fair."

"You're wanting to settle, you claim, so why are you pursuing me?"

Nerves settled in her belly because she wasn't sure she was ready for the answer he would give. This was moving too fast, or perhaps they'd been headed this way for years and she was just catching up.

"Maybe I haven't considered anyone else. Maybe I want to know what a relationship with my best friend would be like." He moved closer as the lights flickered once again. "Maybe I believe that we could have something special, something beyond what we both expect or imagine."

Piper swallowed, holding his gaze. "What about love?"

Ryan froze for a second, then raked his hand down his face. "Piper, you know I want marriage and the whole thing my parents had. I know they were a minority when it came to eternal love, but I'm not sure that's what I feel right now. All I can do is move forward and hope that's what happens. I can't guarantee anything and I'm not making promises."

Piper reached up, cupped his cheek and stroked his dark

stubble with her thumb. She knew he didn't love her, not like a man would love a woman romantically. He loved her on a friend level and that was fine because she herself wasn't sure about that intimate degree of love. Did it even exist? Certainly not for her parents. So how would she know if she was making a mistake if she and Ryan moved forward?

"I can't think about settling down, Ryan. I like my life. I enjoy my work, fixing up my house, hanging with you and watching our friends fall in love and marry."

Ryan reached up, grasped her hand and squeezed. "I'm not asking for wedding bands here, Red. I just want you to know I'm not going anywhere and I plan on seducing you at every opportunity I get. If anything else comes into the mix, then that's icing on the proverbial cake."

Shivers raced through Piper as another loud rumble of thunder shook her old house. The electricity flickered once, twice and finally died.

Silence surrounded them; darkness enveloped them as they stood still holding on to each other.

"Looks like no work for us," he murmured. "I think fate just handed us a prime opportunity."

Piper inhaled Ryan's familiar scent as fear was replaced by certainty. This was the one man who knew her better than anyone. Why shouldn't she let him possess her body, as well? She'd slept with two men in her life, neither of whom she had feelings half as strong for. Ryan was it for her. No, she wasn't ready for marriage or kids, but intimacy with the one man who always made her feel safe and cherished, and treated her like a lady would not be a wrong decision.

"I'm tired of being strong for both of us." She searched his eyes, praying she was making the right decision. "I'm tired of analyzing this to death and I'm tired of this achiness I feel when I'm around you. I can't handle it anymore."

Ryan slid both hands around her face and into her hair, pulling her closer. "Piper, I don't want to pressure you. Be sure about this. I'm demanding and I don't want you to regret this later."

"I'll have no regrets," she told him, knowing she wouldn't. "I want you. I want what's started between us. I know you in so many ways, but not the most important one. I want to know more, Ryan. Show me more."

Ryan's lips came down fast and hard on hers. He claimed her as he never had before. His tongue thrusting in and out as his hips aligned with hers had Piper moaning and gripping his shoulders.

Rain beat down on the house, thunder rattled the old windows. Storms had always been sexy to her. The intrigue, the careless manner in which they came through, the loss of control. Much like sex.

The ambience couldn't have been better scripted for their first time. With their playful bickering through the years and the way they'd met, with her quick punch to his face as kids, the thunderstorm sweeping through was almost nostalgic, like Mother Nature echoing their own stormy relationship.

Perhaps Fate had planned this whole evening. Who was she to argue?

Ryan gripped her shirt and tugged it from her work pants. With little finesse, he jerked it apart, sending the tiny buttons flying across the room, spattering as they hit the wall, the floor. Piper didn't care that he was in such a hurry. She knew the need he had because that same urge burned in her, stronger than she ever thought possible.

"Wish I'd worn something a little more feminine," she told him.

Hunger stared back at her. "I don't want you any other way, Piper. Always remember that."

Strong hands encircled her waist, his thumbs stroked along the underside of her breasts across the lacy edge of her bra.

"Perfectly feminine," he whispered. "Perfectly mine."

As shivers raced through her, Piper went to work on his pants. In no time Ryan had released her, shucked his work boots and jeans, leaving his glorious body in only black boxer briefs. Seeing this man in swimming trunks was hot, but this was downright scorching with his erection trying to spring free out the top of his boxers. Ryan Grant should pose for one of those hot, hunky cowboy calendars. The world really shouldn't be deprived of seeing this tatted-up bad boy in nothing but his Stetson and snug briefs.

"I wish I could see you in the light," she muttered. "I feel cheated."

"Surely you have candles."

Piper started to turn away, but Ryan caught her arm.

"Take off your pants. I want to watch you walk away so I can see everything I've been wanting for months."

"Months?"

Ryan nipped at her lips and whispered, "Years."

Piper had no idea she'd held such control over him and she knew he wasn't just saying this. Ryan had had his fair share of buckle bunnies, but he'd never flaunted it and never acted like his ego had become inflated because of it.

And the fact that he could have nearly any woman he wanted and he'd wanted her for so long only made her all the more anxious to be with him.

Piper unlaced her work boots and kicked them off, shoved her pants around her ankles and kicked them aside, as well.

Even in the dark, Piper could see Ryan's eyes widen as

they slid down her body. Anticipation swirled inside her, sending shivers shooting throughout her body.

"You better hurry up if you want those candles," he told her, his voice husky.

Piper turned toward her bedroom where she had a large fat candle on her nightstand. She grabbed it and the matches in the drawer and hurried back, careful not to bang her toe on the end of her bed. The darkness could be sexy, but bashing yourself before foreplay could even begin would not be a turn-on. They'd had enough injuries between them.

When she turned, Ryan stood in the doorway, then moved toward her. Apparently this intimate party was getting started.

Piper set the candles on her dresser and lit them; the room soon basked into a soft, radiant glow.

Ryan eased forward, sliding his hands around her waist, then to her back, and dipped his fingertips in the top of her lacy panties.

The gentle light from the flickering candle set the perfect scene and she could so appreciate his body all the more. The ink that swirled around his left pec and up over his shoulder intrigued her. She'd never given the tat much thought before, but now she found it sexy, alluring, as it stretched across his taut muscle.

"Seeing your panties hanging in your bathroom a few weeks ago nearly killed me, Red. I instantly imagined what you'd look like in them. I knew you'd be smokin' hot. But even my imagination didn't come close to reality."

Roaming her hands up his chiseled biceps and over his shoulders, Piper smiled. "I'm glad you're not disappointed. I don't want this to be awkward, Ryan."

His hands moved into her panties and cupped her bottom, jerking her toward his erection.

Ryan's shadowed face inched closer to hers; he licked his lips and hoisted her up off the floor. Piper wrapped her legs around his waist, her arms looped around his neck. His chest hair tickled her breasts.

"I've waited so long for this," he whispered. "I want to memorize every moment, but mostly I want to be inside you. I want to know how you feel around me. I want to see you lose control again and know that I'm the cause of your recklessness."

Who knew her best friend had such a sexy bedroom voice? And who knew he'd had these thoughts about her for so long? Had she missed the subtle hints or had he kept his emotions and fantasies hidden on the inside?

"Then why are we still talking?" she asked. "Take what you want, cowboy."

His wide smile melted her and she sank her fingers into his messy hair and pulled his mouth against hers.

With only their underwear separating every aching part, Piper rocked her hips against his as her tongue swept inside his mouth, seeking more contact. She just couldn't get close enough.

Ryan walked backward until her back hit the wall.

"I want all of you, Piper," he murmured against her lips. Sweat dampened their bodies.

"Since the fans won't work without electricity, maybe a cool shower will help us."

Piper grinned against his lips. "I doubt we'll cool off, but the thought of getting you naked and wet is one of the best ideas you've had."

"I try." He laughed.

He eased her down his body until her feet hit the cool tile. She slid out of her panties and unclasped her bra, flinging it aside. When she glanced back up, Ryan was watching her, his lids heavy, his gaze on her body as if he were looking at her for the very first time.

"The word *want* seems like such an understatement right now," he murmured. "Crave, desire, hunger for…"

Feeling a bit more flirtatious, she was naked after all, Piper held her arms wide. "Then take what you want, Ryan. I'm not afraid. Once won't be enough and I can't guarantee slow or gentle."

His eyes came back up to hers. "If you knew what I want from you, you would be afraid."

"There's nothing you can do to scare me away," she told him, easing closer. "I know you, inside and out. And if you'd shut up, I could get to know you a whole lot more."

In one swift move, Ryan lifted her up walked into the newly renovated bathroom. Thankfully she'd washed the dust out of the shower last night so she could see the tile work.

Holding on to Piper, he stepped over the small tiled edge into the wide, open shower with nozzles on each of the side walls. This was one area she'd refused to skimp on and, man, she was so glad she had put in the extra cash for this luxurious, oversize shower.

Water slid over her body as Ryan reached up and tugged on her hair. Piper stepped aside, pulled the rubber band loose and flung it out of the shower. Ryan took both hands, shaking out her day's worth of sloppy ponytail and tilted her head so her hair became soaked from the spray.

Closing her eyes, Piper relished the moment of being held, cherished, pampered and even loved by her best friend in a way she never thought possible. There was nothing awkward or weird about their coming together. If anything, being naked in the shower with Ryan was a level of perfection she'd never experienced in her life.

Piper held on to his arms and lifted her head. Water

dripped into her face and Ryan eased down, using his lips to capture the droplets on her forehead, her cheeks, her lips. Cupping both breasts, he sank to his knees and kissed her flat stomach.

"I've never seen a more beautiful sight," he said, looking back up at her. "I'd stay on my knees forever for you, Piper."

Damn, why did he have to say things like that? She didn't want the whole of forever to enter into this. She wanted sex. That's all. She didn't know if this would work and bringing another complication into the mix made her uncomfortable. For now, she needed to concentrate on the fact that she was about to make love to Ryan.

Before she could reply, he kissed her stomach again, his hands roaming down her waist and settling at her hips. Instinct had her spreading her legs wide, placing her hands on his wet, muscular shoulders.

Ryan kissed her belly button and made a path down until he was at her center where she ached the most. Strong hands gripped her hips as he kissed her inner thighs, one agonizing inch at a time.

Piper looked down, wanting to see him, knowing the erotic image they made, and the knowledge of what he was about to do turned her on even more. This was a giant step beyond making love and she couldn't do a thing to stop him. She'd lost all control over this situation—perhaps she never had it to begin with. Ryan literally held her in the palm of his hands.

He used his thumbs to spread her apart and he took no time in gliding his tongue across her. Piper's knees nearly buckled, but his hold on her hips tightened as he made love to her with his mouth.

Easing back, Piper rested against the tile next to the pulsing spray. She needed more, so much more, but she didn't know what or even how to ask. Every part of her screamed for release, yet she didn't want it to end too soon. She could hardly control herself and she wanted to remember this moment.

As if Ryan knew what she needed, he slid a hand down her leg and took her foot, placing it on the small bench along the back wall of the shower. Exposed as she was, Piper felt sensations she never knew were possible with her body. She'd certainly never experienced anything like this before.

Her hips pumped; her hands went into Ryan's hair, his shoulders, anywhere she could reach because the turmoil her body was going through was driving her insane. She needed… She didn't know what she needed. Faster, slower, harder. Something to make this ache subside.

Ryan eased a finger inside her and…yes. That was it. Piper jerked her hips against him as her body tightened and the climax slammed into her. Ryan continued his assault with his mouth and hand until her shivers ceased.

But when he looked up her body at her, Piper heated all over again.

"You're the sexiest woman I've ever seen," he told her, coming to his feet and leaning his full length against her body. "I can't wait, Piper. I need you now. We can do slow later."

Later. She liked the sound of that. One word held so much promise and the fact they were just getting started sent thrills of excitement through her.

The flickering of the candlelight combined with the cool temperature of the shower and the added effects from Mother Nature had Piper wishing this unexpected night would never end.

Ryan kissed her shoulder, moving his way across to her neck, then down to take one nipple into his mouth. Piper wasn't sure what else he had in mind, but her body was still humming and she didn't know how much longer she was going to have to wait.

Time to take charge.

She shoved him back and smiled. Placing a hand on his chest, she eased him back until his legs came in contact with the tiled bench. Ryan sank onto it and Piper settled one knee on either side of his hips.

Ryan leaned back against the wall. "This is a view I could get used to, as well."

Piper laughed. "You have a boob fetish."

"I'm a guy."

Piper started to sink down onto him, but Ryan gripped her waist and halted her progress.

"Condom?" he asked.

Piper closed her eyes and groaned. "I don't have any."

He nipped at her lips. "I've never gone without one and I have regular physicals."

"Same here," she panted. "And I'm on birth control."

His eyes sought hers. "I want to feel you. Only you."

"Please," she begged.

"I want to remember this, Piper. I don't want you to forget this moment."

Her eyes locked on to his. "As if I could."

She captured his lips as she sank down, consuming him in so many ways. He filled her, more than she'd initially thought he would and Piper took a moment to adjust.

"Okay?" he asked, his forehead resting against hers.

Piper nodded as she started moving, slowly at first, then faster. Ryan continued to grip her hips as his mouth found her breast. She braced her hands on the wall behind his head and pumped her body faster because another wave of glorious pleasure was building and she wanted to take him with her this time.

Piper shut her eyes, bit her lip, but nothing could hold back the scream as another climax took over.

Beneath her, Ryan stilled as he tilted his head back against the wall. The muscle in his jaw clenched and Piper rode out her pleasure with him. His body tightened and Piper had never seen a more glorious sight than Ryan giving in to total bliss and abandonment.

And when she wrapped her arms around his neck, rested her head on his shoulder, she let the cool shower beat down on her because she knew this night of passion was just getting started.

Twelve

Piper lay across her bed, sweaty, sated and sore. Mercy sakes, that man knew how to deliver on a promise. When he'd said he'd been thinking about intimacy with her for years she'd kind of laughed it off, but after that performance, she was inclined to believe him. That man had skills she'd never experienced before.

There wasn't a part of her body he hadn't touched either with his hands or his soft words. Piper would be lying if she didn't admit her heart had been just as involved as her body during their lovemaking last night. Getting tangled up with Ryan was something she certainly hadn't planned on, but there was no way she could've fought off the desire, the passion, any longer.

And now that her heart was becoming more immersed, she knew she had to watch every step she took in this new relationship. The last thing she could handle was losing his friendship. He'd been her rock, her sounding board and her fun-time friend for twenty years. Nothing could break her more than losing that solid foundation in her life.

The electricity still hadn't returned and she was going to have to fire up her generator so she could turn on her box fans or she'd end up in a cold shower again…not that the first round was bad.

She started to pull away from the dead weight of Ryan's

thick, muscular arm across her bare torso. She loved the feel of him on her, around her, in her. Who knew her best friend had such mad skills in the bedroom? No wonder all those buckle bunnies were traipsing after him at every event.

The man could ride without fear and never break a sweat. He was cool under pressure, but when it came to the bedroom, Ryan Grant was anything but laid-back. The man was in control, dominant and sexy as hell. The way he silently demanded affection… The way he so selflessly pleasured her over and over again… Piper was utterly ruined for any other man.

And how in the world could she ever go back to being just his friend? Yeah, that would never happen. No way could she look at him, talk to him, eat a meal with him and not recall the way he'd made her feel, the way he'd looked at her as he moved within her.

"Where are you going?" he mumbled, half his face squished into the wrinkled sheet.

"Just going to start the generator so I can get the fans moving some of this hot air."

"Why don't we go take another shower?" he said, eyes heavy and locking on to hers. "Or better yet, let's just go to my house. I probably have electricity."

"That was a nasty storm, Ryan. The streetlights were still out last night, so I imagine the town is out."

He lifted up onto an elbow and rested his head on the palm of his hand. "Yeah, but I live outside of town so maybe I didn't get hit as hard."

Piper eased up in bed, lacing her hand through his. "You have a problem staying here?"

In a swift move, he snaked his arm around her waist and pulled her back down. "Maybe I just want you in my bed."

The heat in his eyes this morning was just as intense as

she'd seen last night. She'd been worried that, come daylight, some of his enthusiasm for their newfound intimacy would've died down, but apparently not.

Yeah, she was so ruined for any other man. God help her.

"Don't make this weird, Red." He raked his thumb across her nipple. "We're just much better friends now."

"Well, I can honestly say I've never slept with a friend before, so this is uncharted territory for me."

"I've never slept with a friend before, either, but I'm sure as hell glad you were my first."

Piper laughed. "And here I didn't think you had any *firsts* left."

"I think you used up the last one." He chuckled, still fondling her breast. "I need you to know, I'm more than aware of how the media portrayed me through the years—my personal life on the road—but you surely know that I didn't sleep with every woman that slithered my way or that I was photographed with."

Piper held up a hand before he could speak. "We've been friends so long, Ryan, I know you're not one to sleep around. But I really don't want to hear about what you did or didn't do with those buckle bunnies."

He grabbed her hands, all joking aside as he searched her face. "No, it's important to me that you don't see me as some man-whore. I can count on one finger the number of one-night stands I've had on the road and I can count on my whole hand the number of women I've slept with... and that includes you."

Piper couldn't stop her gasp, nor could she stop her mouth from dropping open. "You don't have to say this."

"Yes, I do. I never cared what people thought about my sex life, the media will say what they want anyway." He squeezed her hands. "But I care what you think. I care now even more because of this."

Piper didn't want to delve too deeply into why it was so important for him to share all his bedroom romps now. She didn't want to think that maybe he was truly giving up the circuit and settling down. He'd made great progress with the school, which gave her hope that her best friend was indeed staying, but what if he got that itch to travel again? What if he decided that the adventure of home life wasn't enough?

What if he left like her father always had?

"Let's throw on the bare minimum of clothes and head to my place," he suggested, cutting into her thoughts. "It's quieter out there and there's more privacy. We can run naked through the house and no neighbors are around to see. Well, there are all the animals I have now, but they won't say anything."

Piper swatted his bare shoulder. "You're pathetic. I can't just be naked all day, Ryan. I have things to do."

"Like what? I know you're off today and with the electricity out, there's not much you can do on your house."

The man would tempt the devil himself. How could Piper say no when her body was already responding to him, already eagerly awaiting what talented moves he had yet to show her.

And in his bed? Piper would love nothing more than to wake up in his bed tomorrow morning, but how long would that last?

Her cell rang, breaking the intimacy.

"Let it go to voice mail," he told her.

"I can't, Ryan. It may be work or any number of people who need me. It would have to be important considering how early it is."

"I need you," he said, grabbing for her as she scooted off the bed. "I'll hold your place and I expect you to come back."

Piper smiled and went to her dresser to retrieve her cell. Cara's name popped up on the screen.

"Cara?" Piper answered. "Is everything okay?"

"It's fine," Cara told her. "I'm sorry to bother you so early, Piper."

"Is it Alex?" Piper asked, glancing across the room at Ryan who had now sat up in bed, the sheet pooling around his tanned waist.

"He's fine. I mean, he's the same," she clarified. "That's what's bothering me. I went to his house this morning, like I've been doing, to check on him. He's always been such an early riser, and I brought his favorite muffins. Anyway, after that bad storm, I was worried about him and I just keep hoping one morning I'll pop in and he'll tell me he's remembered."

Aware that she was standing completely naked, Piper crossed the room to her bath where she pulled her short, silky robe from the back of the door. Juggling the cell, she slid into the thin garment.

"Cara, it will take time," Piper assured her friend. "Don't be discouraged. You're doing everything you can to jog his memory."

"He has a wonderful life waiting on him," Cara went on. "I just want some answers. He's so frustrated and there's nothing I can do to help."

"Have you shown him more pictures?" Piper asked.

"We've looked at so many pictures. I'm at a loss now." Cara sighed. "I even asked him about having a barbecue with all of our friends in hopes that it would help to be surrounded by familiar faces, but he refused. He said he's just not ready for all of the questions and the pity. I understand that, but I just can't sit by and do nothing."

"You're not doing nothing, Cara. You're there every day. He's seeing your face over and over, and pretty soon he'll start having flashes of seeing you before the accident. And hopefully before long he'll remember what happened and we can put this nightmare behind us."

"I went pretty far in trying to jog his memory," Cara almost whispered. "When the pictures weren't doing anything, I…"

Piper waited, but her friend was silent. "Cara?"

"Never mind." Cara sighed. "I'm sorry to bother you, Piper. I just… I didn't know who to call and you've been so good to me through this. I have to be strong for him and occasionally I need to vent."

"I'm always here, Cara. Day or night."

"Thanks. I just needed to talk. I know we don't know each other really well, but I feel like we formed a bond after the accident." Cara sighed. "I guess I needed someone not so close to the situation. But Alex and I are going to get through this. I won't let him get away again. We have a life to plan together."

Piper grinned. "That's the kind of attitude you need, Cara. That strength will get you both through this."

Piper hung up and laid her phone back on the dresser.

"Alex okay?" Ryan asked.

Piper made her way back over to the bed. "He's the same. I think the lack of change is about to tear Cara down. She's really been so strong and holding it together. But there's only so much the poor woman can take."

Ryan reached for her hand and eased her down beside him. "She's got friends and family, and when Alex returns from whatever prison his mind is in, she will be fine."

"I hope so. She's so scared for him. She's not even feeling sorry for herself, she just wants to help him."

"I know another strong woman like that," Ryan said, toying with the ends of her hair.

God, her hair. She couldn't even imagine the mess it was in this morning after the shower, then air drying without product, then rolling around in the bed. Good thing Ryan was the man she'd woken up to. He'd seen her at her worst before and apparently he was fine with it.

Yes, there were perks to sleeping with your best friend. All the awkward moments were out of the way.

"If you keep looking at me like that, we won't make it to my house," he told her, his voice low, husky.

He pulled the silk ties of her robe until they slid loose, then he parted it as he ran his fingertips up from her abdomen to her breasts. Piper allowed the robe to slide back off her shoulders and land behind her on the bed.

"Who says we have to leave right now?" she asked. "I'm kinda hungry."

His eyes roamed over her chest and back up. "You have the best ideas."

Leaning back, Piper smiled. "Literally. I'm hungry."

She leaped out of bed, totally naked and not ashamed. He'd seen her, tasted her, why be shy now? Besides, she had plans for him later so getting dressed would be a waste of time.

Piper padded to the kitchen, knowing Ryan wouldn't be far behind. A naked female walking in the opposite direction? Yeah, he was a man. He'd follow.

As she pulled open the cabinet, a sensational, glorious thought crossed her mind. She turned to see Ryan in all his tanned naked cowboy glory standing directly behind her.

"Whatever naughty thought put that look in your eye, I like it," he said, grinning.

"Why don't you go back into the bedroom and wait for me." She shoved at his chest. "Or go into the living room. I'll start the generator and we can close those blinds."

He moved closer, stroking a hand down her face, her shoulder and the slope of her bare breast. "If you take too long, I'm coming after you and I won't care what room you're in."

Arousal shot through her and all she could do was nod. Yeah, he may say she had power over him, but since that first orgasm he'd given her on her porch, he pretty much had her trapped in a lust-filled haze and she wasn't sure she even wanted to get out.

"How about I go fire up the generator while you take care of whatever plans you have," he told her. "You have five minutes and I'll meet you in the living room."

He left her alone and Piper had to force herself to get back to the task she'd started before his heart-stopping nakedness nearly paralyzed her.

Turning back to the cabinet, she pulled out a variety of items. Piper wanted to explore a playful, fun side of sex with Ryan and hoped it would add to their pleasure.

Not surprisingly, she beat him into the living room and arranged her items on the old trunk she'd found at an antique shop. She smiled when he stepped into the room and took in her inventory, including his favorite food.

"If you're thinking what I think you are, I may have just died and gone to heaven," he told her.

"Get that fine butt over here, cowboy."

Feeling flirty and aroused, she couldn't wait to have playful sex. That, she could handle. It was the emotional, intense, slow sex that terrified her. Because she was hanging on by a very thin thread on a very slippery rope and it would only take one slip for her to fall headfirst in love with her best friend.

"I hope those mini marshmallows are for me."

She laughed. "You know I keep them here just for you."

"And what do you plan to do with them?"

Her eyes drifted down his lean, muscular body. "Lay on the couch and you'll find out."

Heat flared in his eyes as he did what she suggested. She knew he was loving every minute of this.

Once he was in position, all stretched out on the length of her sofa, she grabbed a handful of marshmallows and laid them one by one from the middle of his chest, down to his pelvic area.

"Don't move," she told him. "I'd hate to have to start over because one fell off."

His eyes darted to hers. "If these are my favorite, shouldn't I be eating them off of you?"

"You will." She went to her knees beside him, slid her tongue out and snatched the first one from his chest. "When I'm done."

His nostrils flared as she bent to suck off another one. Each time she snatched a marshmallow, he froze as if he were afraid to move, afraid she'd stop. By the time she got to the last one, he was near panting, his fists clenched at his sides.

Piper reached out to stroke him, but in a swift move, he was sitting up and looming over her.

"You're done," he growled. "Now get on the couch and let me return the favor."

Piper stared up at him in shock. "But I'd barely gotten started."

"And if you keep stroking me like that, we'll be done before I can have my fun."

Yeah, she had the control. They both knew it, which made her grin widen.

"I'll return the favor, Ryan." She leaned up, her mouth nearly touching his. "That's a promise and it'll happen when you least expect it."

"You'll be the death of me, Red. But I'll die a happy, satisfied man."

Piper laughed and squealed when he stood, hoisted her to her feet and nearly threw her on the sofa.

"Now it's your turn to see how well you can lay still."

Her body shivered at the promise, the anticipation. They'd always been competitive and she refused to let him win this little foreplay contest.

Ryan reached around, grabbed a handful of marshmallows and popped them into his mouth.

"That's not how you play," she told him, laughing.

"You play your way, I'll play mine."

Piper rolled her eyes. "Am I just going to lay here while you eat?"

His eyes roamed over her, heating her body just the same as if he'd touched her with his bare hands. "Hell, yeah, you are."

She realized her choice of wording may not have been the best, but the thought of Ryan between her thighs only made her all the more anxious.

"What else do we have here?" he said, glancing over at the trunk. "Oh, a little bit of chocolate sauce. This could be fun."

Piper stared at him as he placed one marshmallow at a time in a heart shape on her abdomen. The urge to squirm consumed her and he'd barely touched her. But she had to remain firm.

He popped the top of the chocolate sauce and slowly drizzled it in the outline of the heart.

"Hard to remain still, isn't it?" he asked, a naughty smirk spreading across his kissable mouth. "I promise to make it worth your while."

Piper shivered. She may just lose this little challenge, after all. But with the way his hands and mouth were roaming over her, she knew she'd still be coming out a winner.

Thirteen

"That's it," Ryan said encouragingly. "You've got him."

Will, a senior in high school, was just one of the boys participating in Ryan's program. He needed to get a feel for what worked, what didn't and what he could improve on before fully opening his school. This was a win-win for both him and the boys he had coming after school for a few hours a day.

Ryan climbed down off the chutes as Will headed for the gate. A ranch hand had herded the bull out of the arena already and was off to take care of the animals. Will had been trying his skills on several of the horses and broncs for the past week. From Will's performance today, Ryan was impressed by what he'd seen. This was a young boy who had been brought up learning the ropes and knowing how to handle most animals.

Ryan almost felt like a proud papa.

"You did really well," Ryan told the boy. "You're more than welcome to come out tomorrow even though it's Saturday. I'll be around if you'd like to continue your work."

Will nodded, adjusting his hat lower on his head. "Thanks, Mr. Grant. I'd like that."

Ryan slapped him on the back. "I've told you to call me Ryan. I really think you'll be a great asset to this school and I'd like to offer you a full-time position here for the summer once you're done with school."

Will's eyes widened. "That would be great, Mr.—uh, Ryan."

Ryan headed toward the tack room in the barn as Will moved toward the door. "I'll see you in the morning, Will."

Once he was alone in the barn, Ryan set his music to Metallica and attempted to unwind and relax. Nothing like a little vintage hard rock to round out his day. He usually didn't play music with anyone else here because no one appreciated his fine selection.

Well, he would play it around Piper, but she was special. She hated his music, and he found it amusing to drive her out of her mind as often as possible. And now that they'd shared a bed, numerous times, he'd found a new way to drive her out of her mind.

Barely a week had passed since the storm and since he'd brought her to his house to stay. Having Piper in his bed was exactly where he wanted to keep her. He wanted that extra layer of bonding and he knew she'd felt a connection being on his turf, too. She wanted to hide from any stronger emotions, but he wouldn't allow it.

As he was putting the rest of the equipment away, his cell vibrated in his pocket. Ryan pulled it out and checked the screen.

"Hey, Joe," he greeted his former roping partner.

"Ryan. What's up, ol' buddy?"

Taking a seat on the edge of the tack box, Ryan smiled. "Not much. Just got finished working with a boy who's helping with my school. There's some potential. Reminds me of me when I was a teen."

Joe sighed. "So you're really settling down there, huh?"

"I really am."

"I was hoping you'd be home for a bit and get the itch to get back out into the action."

Action? Yeah, he was getting all the action he could handle with Piper. The circuit didn't even compare.

"I'm staying in Royal," Ryan confirmed. "I'm pretty excited about opening the new school and settling roots in my hometown."

"You'll be great at it, Ryan."

The hesitation in his friend's voice had Ryan coming to his feet. "Joe? Something wrong?"

"I was hoping I could talk you into finishing this season with me."

"What?" Ryan asked, switching the phone to his other ear. "What happened to Dallas?"

"When Dallas replaced you he was on fire, but he broke his leg earlier this week when we were doing practice runs. Snapped his femur when he dismounted and landed wrong. We desperately need you back, man."

Finish the season? Put his school on hold for a little longer than anticipated?

Put Piper on hold?

"How soon would you need an answer?"

God, was he even contemplating this now that he was within reach of everything he'd wanted for his retirement? School, ranch…Piper.

"By tomorrow at the latest," Joe told him. "It would just be for a few more months. Then you can be out for good. You know I wouldn't ask if I didn't really need you."

"Why can't you ask someone else?"

Joe sighed. "I need the money, Ryan. I'm afraid if I don't win this championship we're going to lose our ranch."

Guilt weighed heavy on him. For a cowboy to lose his ranch, well, that was like taking the breath from his lungs. Ryan knew Joe had fallen on hard times recently with personal issues back home and there was no way Ryan could ignore his friend.

But this was a big step and one he'd really have to consider.

"I wouldn't have called if it hadn't been an emergency," Joe told him.

"I know." Ryan sighed. "Let me call you back."

"I knew I could count on you."

"I haven't said yes, yet."

"You will."

Joe disconnected the call and Ryan tossed the phone onto the tack box. Back on the circuit. It was like a drug pulling at him and he hadn't even realized he'd needed a fix. That craving for the adrenaline rush, the instant gratification of being part of a team, of winning, of conquering that damn bull that no one else could.

Every aspect of rodeo had always given him a high like nothing else…made him feel like he could do anything, gave him bragging rights that made him feel as though nothing could hold him back.

Ryan blew out a breath, cranked the heavy metal music even louder and headed outside to stack the hay bales. A little manual labor was what he needed to think, to really focus on what was best for him at this point in his life. But how could he focus on what was best for him when he now thought of himself as a team with Piper?

The late-afternoon sun beat down on him and Ryan reached behind his back and stripped his shirt off, hanging it over the post. Even though it was November, the weather was a bit on the warm side and he'd already worked up a sweat.

He pulled the worn leather gloves from his back pocket and slid them on and went to the stack of hay bales. One after another he tugged, tossed and stacked into the barn. In no time he'd gotten a good sweat worked up and his muscles were screaming. Unfortunately he was no closer to the answer Joe needed.

He'd been so confident when he'd decided to leave the circuit. He'd won nearly every championship, experienced the traveling, the ups and downs, broken bones and mouthfuls of dirt after being bucked. He'd been interviewed and flashed all over the television and every other media outlet.

When he'd walked away, he'd left knowing he'd dedicated years of his life to working, playing and living hard.

Ryan had left knowing the time had come to move on to another chapter, to settle down. Piper was a perk.

If Joe only needed him for the end of this one season, there would be no harm. Ryan hadn't exactly set a date for the school opening and he'd definitely be back by summer seeing as how it was only November. He'd be back by early spring at the absolute latest.

But was the choice to go just selfish on his part? Maybe a little, but he wasn't committing to staying on again or coming out of retirement. He was helping a friend in a desperate time. He knew Joe and Dallas had been winning and were close to the championship. If Ryan didn't step in and help Joe, all his friend's hard work would be for naught.

Ryan truly felt the pull, and not the pull to thrive on that adrenaline rush, but the pull to help his friend, to be able to do everything in his power to get that championship for him.

Another bale stacked and Ryan turned to see Piper holding the water hose, aiming it directly at him. The song in the background switched to Metallica's "The Struggle Within"…fitting for the abrupt turmoil.

He hadn't even heard her come up, which just indicated how loud he'd had his music and how deep in thought he'd been. He had no idea why she was here, but she had that rotten grin on her face and he knew he was in for it.

"I stopped by to see how the school was progressing, but then you were all shirtless and I thought maybe you could use cooling off." She tipped her head and her grin spread even wider. "Looking a little sweaty, cowboy."

He hooked his thumbs in his belt loops and grinned. "Try it. I guarantee you'll only get one shot before I'm on you and there will be repercussions for your naughtiness."

Piper bit her lip, then shrugged. "It's worth it."

The water hit him square in the chest, soaking him and sending water sluicing into his jeans. Ryan dodged the spray by making a hard right and running directly toward her. She'd just turned the hose back on him when he tackled her and sent her flying into a pile of hay. He wrestled the hose away from her and doused her.

That pale pink T-shirt she'd been wearing now molded to her every curve, outlining firm breasts and erect nipples.

Perhaps the torture was all on him, after all. Not that he would ever complain about seeing Piper in a wet T-shirt.

With hands up to protect her face, Piper laughed and came to her feet. Ryan let go of the nozzle, still holding on to the hose in case she decided to attack again.

"Give up?" he asked, staring directly at her chest and not caring if that was rude.

"I'll never admit defeat." She laughed as she walked toward him. "But you do look much cooler."

He tossed the hose aside and snaked an arm around her waist, hauling her against his chest. "I'm anything but cool."

Her eyes widened, then fell to his mouth. "Are we all alone in here?"

"Except for the animals, but I assure you, they don't care."

Ryan's hands slid up over her soaked shirt. When he

molded his hands around her breasts, she sighed, arching into him.

"And here I was just stopping by to see if you wanted dinner."

Ryan leaned forward, licked a droplet of water from her neck. "Yeah, I do," he whispered. "But I don't think we're suitable to be in public. Shame that."

He attacked her mouth. There was no finesse, no control. Only hot need to have her naked. Now.

There wasn't a time since they'd become intimate that he didn't want her. She looked like a walking fantasy right now and there was no way he could let her go without having her. The barn wasn't the most romantic place, but he'd pretty much killed the romance when he decided to have sex with her with blaring heavy metal for mood music.

Ryan backed her up to the saddle stand and eased her down to sit. In no time he'd pulled her shirt from her jeans and pried it up and over her head. The bra came next and then Ryan closed his mouth over one taut peak as Piper groaned and fisted her hands in his hair. Somewhere between the hose and the tackle he'd lost his Stetson.

The thought of being out in the open barn where anyone driving up could see them only added to his arousal. He needed her and everything else be damned.

Piper clutched at his shoulders, groaning as he licked, tugged and flicked her nipples with his tongue.

"Enough." She shoved him back, coming to her feet and reaching for his belt. "I want more."

"Here?" he asked, smiling at her control, her sudden dominance.

"Here, now and fast." She unfastened his wet jeans, then started tugging them down. "Think you can handle it, cowboy?"

Oh, he could handle it, but what he couldn't handle were

these damn wet jeans. The dead last thing he needed was restrictions for what he had in mind.

He kept his around his ankles and assisted her in ridding herself of her worn cowboy boots and wet jeans. That bright white thong was torn off in about a second and he spun her around.

"Brace your hands on the saddle," he whispered in her ear. "I've always wanted you like this."

"Then quit talking about it and do—"

He slammed into her from behind before she could finish her sentence. Yeah, tight and hot just as he'd imagined. Every single time with Piper was like the first. He never got used to the emotions, the euphoria that enveloped him. And he hoped to hell he never got used to how perfect they were together.

She leaned forward, tilting her hips higher, taking him deeper. Ryan clutched at her hips, afraid he'd bruise her if he held on as tightly as he truly wanted.

As he pumped in and out of her, he slid one hand up to palm a breast.

"Ryan," she panted. "Oh…"

That's right. His was the only name that would be on her lips if he had any say.

"You're so damn sexy," he said. "I can't get enough."

"Me, either."

Between her wet body bent over the saddle stand and her tight center, Ryan knew he was close. But Piper started jerking her hips faster, squeezing his hand tighter and within seconds she was contracting around him.

Ryan couldn't hold back another second. He pumped one last time and stilled. The climax shook his body, taking control as never before.

Beneath him Piper had rested her head on her arm and was still breathing hard.

When he'd finished trembling, he wrapped both arms around her waist and enveloped her body beneath his. He never wanted to be apart, never wanted this satisfaction to come to an end. But he had a decision to make and he feared her reaction wouldn't be in his favor.

"Did we make it out alive?" she muttered beneath him. "I'm pretty sure I had an out of body experience."

Ryan chuckled. "I feel honored I've made it into a cliché."

"God, that was...yeah."

"You feel so good," he told her, kissing her bare, wet shoulder. "Think we could just stay like this?"

"As long as you don't have anywhere to be or anyone coming for a visit."

"I do have a boy coming for training in the morning."

Beneath him Piper laughed. "I think he may get more schooling than he signed on for if he catches us like this."

Ryan eased up, pulling her with him. "You sure do look hot bent over a saddle stand, Red."

"You cowboys and your fantasies." She slid her arms up around his neck. "But I may have a fantasy or two of my own when it comes to you."

His hands slid down, cupping her bare rear end. "Feel free to use me for any and all fantasies from here on out."

Her eyes widened. "Are you..."

"I'm thinking long-term, Red. You know I want to settle with roots here. I've become a member of the Texas Cattleman's Club, I'm opening a rodeo school in the spring. I'm pretty happy with my life and I'm more than happy with the way we're heading."

"And where are we heading, Ryan?" she asked, her eyes searching his.

"I want to share our relationship," he told her. "We always seem to stay in."

"Because we're always naked," she told him with a smile. "Besides, you took me to Claire's last week."

"Yes, but we've been to Claire's as friends before. I want to take you as my girlfriend."

Piper's smiled widened. "I so wish there was another term for that. I mean, we are thirty and that sounds so high school. But I do love the fact you want to go public."

He kissed her softly, passionately, then pulled back. "Maybe public can wait till tomorrow. I'd rather work on some of those fantasies you had in mind."

Ryan led her to the tack room where he closed the door. He wanted to enjoy tonight. He wanted to spend hours of bliss with nothing between them.

Tomorrow he would tell her he'd made up his mind to rejoin the circuit for a few months to help a friend win the championship. He would try his damnedest to persuade her to come along with him and they could still be just as happy on the road.

And while all that sounded perfect in a dream world, Ryan knew he wouldn't be feeling so nervous about telling her if he thought she'd take the news well.

Yeah, his nerves didn't come from the thought of telling her; his unsettled worry stemmed from her reaction. Deep down he knew she would hate this news. But would she hate it enough to stay behind? Would she look beyond the fact he was leaving again and see what they mean to each other?

Morning would come all too soon and he'd have his answer.

Fourteen

Piper stretched. Muscles screamed, but her body had never felt better.

She glanced across the room to the small picture on Ryan's nightstand—a picture of the two of them as kids. Messy, dirty, holey jeans and cowboy hats. Piper smiled as she remembered that day. She'd wanted to impress Ryan and had convinced him to come to her house to meet her dad.

Walker Kindred had snapped a picture of the two of them in front of Piper's mare, Flash. Piper had never been more proud to be the daughter of a rodeo star. But that stardom had certainly come at a price and she and her mother had paid it.

Of course, she couldn't look at that picture and be sad. That was the first picture of her and Ryan together. All these years later he still had it, and in a frame, no less. She was well aware he had random pictures of them together, but knowing he felt this one was worthy of being the only one in his bedroom told her how special that moment was to him, as well. How special she was to him.

How could she deny her feelings? How could she pretend they were still just friends? The man practically worshipped her. He did everything for her, cared for her and had showed her what true friendship was all about. And isn't that how most couples started?

The intimacy with Ryan was amazing and she hoped their new, sexual relationship continued to grow. Dare she hope for something more?

He'd stated he was ready to settle down, ready to move on to the next stage of his life and he'd made it no secret he wanted to try with her.

A piece of her truly hoped this was headed toward something permanent, something…legal. Never before had she envisioned herself married. There were so many marriages popping up around town and she'd been thrilled for each and every couple, but had never once thought this would happen to her.

But now she teetered on the brink of daydreaming about a wedding. She'd want it outside, maybe in the fall with all the beautiful colors of nature surrounding them. A simple dress because she wasn't one to fuss over clothes.

Of course, the time and place didn't matter so long as Ryan was the man at the end of the aisle.

A giggle bubbled up within her. God, now she'd not only started envisioning weddings, she was on the verge of giggling. Could she act more like a teen girl?

But there was something special about moving to another level with her best friend. Piper hoped all married couples experienced a fraction of the happiness she had. Ryan was home, he intended to stay and he'd made an advance with her and their relationship that she'd been terrified of, but she was so glad she'd taken that leap with him.

Rolling over with a smile, she put her hand out and encountered a still-warm sheet. She glanced at the clock. Almost seven. Those rancher cowboys were always up so blasted early.

But the smell of coffee wafted through his house and Piper pulled herself out of bed. She snagged one of his plain white T-shirts from the top of a laundry basket in the corner of his room. After sliding into it, and relishing at the coziness, she padded barefoot down the gleaming hardwood hallway toward the kitchen.

From the doorway she saw him wearing nothing but those low-slung jeans that molded to his backside beautifully, holding a coffee mug and staring out at the barn. The golden sunrise in the distance brightened the room, almost as if a new promise for the day lay ahead for them. There was happiness sliding into her life where there had once been sorrow and void. Ryan had given her hope, had given her a reason to believe again.

Piper tiptoed forward, crossing the room silently, and wrapped her arms around his shoulders. She loved the sexy, masculine scent that always lingered on his skin. Whether it was his soap or cologne, she didn't know.

"Morning," she murmured against his neck. "Have you been up long?"

He reached up, holding on to her arm. "Not really. Couldn't sleep."

"You could've woken me up."

Turning in her arms, he reached to the side and set the mug on the small breakfast table. He wrapped his thick arms around her and pulled her against his bare chest, which had become her favorite place to rest.

"I didn't want to bother you," he told her. "Besides, if I'd woken you in bed and we were both naked, I think you know what would've happened."

Piper peered up at him with a grin. "Would that be so bad?"

He nipped at her lips. "Not at all."

When he eased back, Piper took in the crease between his brows, the tension in his shoulders, the near frown on his devastatingly handsome face. Something weighed heavy on his mind and he was trying to figure it out on his own. She wasn't having any of that.

"What is it?" she asked.

Ryan smoothed a hand over her hair, pushing the way-ward curls away from her face. A fruitless attempt considering her hair was a wreck in the mornings, but he seemed to be agitated or nervous about something. Being on edge was not a quality she'd ever known Ryan to possess, which told her what he hadn't yet…something was wrong.

"Ryan."

"You know I have strong feelings for you."

It wasn't a question, but he didn't sound thrilled about the announcement, either, so Piper just nodded.

"When I say deeper, I mean like I'm pretty sure I'm falling in love with you, Red. I don't take this lightly."

Piper's breath caught. She'd had a feeling, but to hear the words come from his mouth…

"Ryan—"

"Wait—" he held up a hand "—I just need to get this out and then you can have the floor and say anything you need."

Piper nodded and stepped back, giving him space. Apparently whatever he needed to say was going to be life-altering and she needed to be closer to the door…in case she had to make a hasty exit. If he was calling this off, she would be utterly broken.

"When I moved back home I was more than ready to start this school, to become an active member with TCC and to really put down roots in Royal." He raked a hand over his messy bed-head. "I even imagined this, between us. I knew if I could somehow take us beyond our comfort level of being best friends, I was confident we could have something special."

Piper really, really liked what he was saying, but for each second he spoke she waited on the giant "but" that would inevitably come. And if he dashed her dreams, if he was trying to break things off, she would be crushed, heartbroken and shattered. But she had to remain strong for now until she knew what she was facing. So help her, if he decided he'd changed his mind, she'd kick his ass for making her envision a future with him.

"And what we've found is far greater than anything I ever imagined, Piper." He met her gaze and stepped forward. "I want you to know all of that. I want you to understand the level of my feelings for you, the fact that I would die before I ever let anyone or anything hurt you."

Tears pricked her eyes and she blinked them away. She honestly couldn't tell if he was getting ready to propose, tell her he had a fatal disease or if he was breaking up.

"You're scaring me, Ryan. Just say what you need to say. The groundwork has been laid."

Ryan sighed, reaching for her hands and squeezing them. "Joe called me yesterday."

For a moment the name didn't hit her, but when it did, dread settled in the pit of her stomach.

"Your old roping partner," she said slowly. "I'm assuming he wants you back and that's why you had to tell me your feelings so I'd be all mushy and happy on the inside before you delivered this blow."

Okay, so maybe she was jumping the gun and letting her anger seep in just a wee bit. But from the look on his face, she knew she'd nailed it.

Oh, God. The hurt. That instant, piercing pain that enveloped her nearly knocked her to her knees. How dare he do this to her, to them? Especially knowing how she felt about the circuit. Was he seriously just going to jump back in and say to hell with everything else?

"You've got to be kidding." She slid her hands from his and crossed her arms over her chest. "You get one phone call and you're ready to just throw in the towel on everything? The school, your new home and the club? Us?"

"Hear me out before you jump to conclusions."

Piper needed to do something, needed to keep busy so

Ryan wouldn't see her hands shaking…from fear, from anger. She went to the cabinet and pulled down a mug.

"By all means," she said, pouring herself a cup of coffee. "Don't let me stand in the way of your dream. Carry on."

Okay, she was a tad snarky and she'd already put up a wall of anger around her, but damn it, she'd known this could happen. She was more than aware of his love of the rodeo and she'd seen how the circuit got in the blood and became more addictive than drugs. She'd seen firsthand how this damn sport destroyed her family and she would not lay back and play the victim if Ryan chose to leave. This was as much her fault for getting her hopes up, for trusting him when he'd told her time and time again that he wasn't her father.

When she turned and leaned against the counter, her gaze sought his over the top of her mug.

"Joe's new partner that replaced me broke his leg last week," Ryan started, holding her gaze. "They only need me to finish out the season. Two months tops. I don't intend to return permanently, Piper. I hadn't planned on this, either, but Joe needs an answer soon and I can't leave him hanging."

Piper nearly choked on her coffee. Damn, she hated black anyway, but she wasn't breaking the tension by crossing the room for the milk. She needed the anger that enveloped her because if she let go of it, all she'd have left to hold on to would be fear, anguish and a flood of tears she'd be damned if she'd let him see. One had already leaked out, but she'd remain in control for as long as possible. She was a strong woman; she'd lived through rejection before.

"And leaving everything else hanging is something you're comfortable with." She silently commended herself for the iciness she'd been able to lace through her tone.

"That's just it," he told her, stepping toward her. "I don't want to leave anything hanging. My school won't open until spring anyway and I was hoping you'd come with me."

Piper froze, clutching her mug. "You what?"

"I want you to come with me."

"Let me get this straight." She set the mug on the granite countertop behind her and turned back to him, coming to stand at her full height. "You want me to uproot a life I love here, friends I love and friends who need me, just so you can get a few last kicks in?"

"You're not uprooting, Piper. It's two months. And it has nothing to do with my kicks."

She poked his chest. "You're damn right I'm not uprooting. You say two months, but what you really mean is two months now and when next season rolls around maybe a few more then and before you know it, you've gotten sucked back in."

The muscle in Ryan's jaw ticked. Yeah, he may be angry but she was fuming.

"I'm not your father," he said through gritted teeth.

"From where I'm standing you're exactly like him."

Ryan shook his head, placing his hands on his narrow hips. "And that's been hanging between us this whole time, hasn't it? You've been waiting on me to go back. You've been waiting on me to screw up so you could throw your father back in my face. The one man who you trusted as a little girl, the one man who'd let you down. Well, if you want to play that card, fine. I can't stop you, but you damn well know I'm a man of my word, Piper, and when I say I'll be back, I will. It's up to you what you want to do with that information."

"You're right," she agreed. Piper cursed the lone tear that slid down her cheek. So much for control. "But for how long will you be back, Ryan? I can't fault you for loving the rodeo. I can't fault you for wanting to help your friend. But I can fault you for promising me to stay and then expecting me to be happy when you're not. I can fault you for pulling our relationship into something I'd only dreamed of and I can fault you for making me love you. Because I do."

Piper paused, swallowed and wiped at her damp cheek. "God help me, Ryan, I do love you. But I can't wait for you to decide if you're going to stay or go. And I can't just give up my job, my friends, and wait on you to make up your mind on what you truly want because I'm convinced you don't know."

"But I do, Red. I know what I want."

She smiled through the pain. "Yes, you do. It's just that you can't have it all at the same time, so you'll have to choose."

When he remained silent, the fullness he'd placed in her heart shattered and each and every shard sliced into her. Even as he stood with tears brimming in his eyes, she couldn't believe he wasn't backing down. Of course, neither was she, so they were at a standstill.

Pride…it was a fickle emotion that ruined lives.

Running a hand through her mass of curls, Piper nodded. "It's okay. I won't make you say it. I'll get my stuff and be on my way. Go ahead and call Joe."

Piper didn't wait on him to respond, to tell her she was wrong. The entire way back to the bedroom where they'd made love and shared dreams of the future, she waited on him to call her name.

But silence filled the house.

Fifteen

Today wasn't as bad as the past few days at work had been. At least that was a positive in Piper's life.

Alex still hadn't regained his memory. Her house renovations were at a standstill because, well, she'd been spending more and more time at Ryan's house and her priorities had shifted.

Ryan. Even his name made her ache. But she would not give in to the anguish. She'd known his leaving was a very real possibility even though he'd denied it adamantly. She'd seen it before, that confidence in retirement, but all it took was one simple phone call for the two men she'd loved to walk easily out of her life.

Oh, her father had claimed he'd be back, but at that point her mother had had enough and set the divorce in motion. It had been her father's "get out of jail free" card because the man had barely looked back.

Piper couldn't blame Ryan for going back to rodeo. That was the life he knew, craved, loved. After his mother passed, he'd escaped to the circuit and had never known any other way.

Staying home, founding a rodeo school for children was a wonderful idea, but in all reality he probably wasn't ready to hang up his rope just yet.

But by the time he decided to come back to Royal,

would she be available? Would she just keep waiting for a time that may or may not come?

There was no one else she'd ever gotten that close with. And if he chose to sell his ranch, nix the school plans and travel around the country again, Piper would survive. She'd hurt more than she'd ever known possible, but she'd live through it.

Piper pulled into her drive and sighed at the unfamiliar vehicle. A very shiny, very new-looking full-size truck with a nice set of wheels. Who was blocking her garage door? The cost of a truck like that would complete all her necessary renovations, that's for damn sure.

At least the roof was finished, as were the kitchen and bath. And finally, thank you, God, the A/C had been installed. All that was left on the inside was the trim work in the living room. Now she was slowly saving for new siding and stone, but that would be a while down the road.

That's it, she told herself as she grabbed her purse from the seat. Think long term about living in this little bungalow she'd always loved and not long term about Ryan because that window of opportunity had slammed shut when she'd rejected his offer to go on the road.

But that was a depressing thought for another time because there was a man on her porch swing, looking very much like he belonged there.

And it wasn't just any man. It was Walker Kindred, her father.

Piper squared her shoulders and tilted her chin as she hoisted her purse up onto her shoulder. She mentally prepared herself to face the man she used to call Daddy, yet hadn't seen in nearly fifteen years—glimpses on television didn't count.

As she approached the steps he came to his feet, slower

than how she'd remembered him moving, whether from age or caution, she didn't know.

She stared at him, unsure of what to say, and he stared right back. Obviously they were at a standstill, but if he had the courage to make it this far, surely he had the courage to start the conversation and explain what had brought him here after all this time.

Piper tried to tamp down the little girl inside her, the one who'd have given anything to have her father come to her. She was an adult now. She was tougher, but her father had come at a time when she was vulnerable. How many more blows could she take in such a short time?

She started forward, but froze when he spoke.

"You look beautiful."

Piper stopped, her foot on the bottom step. "Well, of all the things I expected you to say, that wasn't it."

He grinned. "I wasn't quite sure what I'd say, either. I had hoped something would come to me once I got here."

Piper remained silent again. She hated the awkward silence, hated that she didn't know how to act, how to feel around the man who'd given her life.

"I wasn't sure when you'd be home," he told her, taking off his white cowboy hat and toying with the edges. "I hope it's okay I waited on your porch."

Piper nodded as awkwardness settled between them. They may be family, but they were total strangers. Seeing as how she never thought this moment would come, Piper was at a loss for words. Well, seeing him brought back all the hurt, so she had words for him, she just thought it best to remain silent and not make this any worse.

Walker shook his head. "It's just so good to see you, Piper Jane. I guess while I was sitting here thinking, I just imagined an innocent teenager pulling up. I forget you're a grown woman."

"I won't get into the fact you could've seen me turn into that woman anytime you chose, but that's in the past." She crossed her arms over her chest, to keep the hurt from seeping in any further. So much for keeping those snarky words bottled inside. "What are you doing here?"

He took a step forward toward the edge of the porch. "I'm here to see you. I have some things to discuss. Is there a time that's good for you?"

Piper looked at him, really looked. His skin was pale, wrinkles fanned out around his eyes and he was thinner than she remembered.

No matter how he'd hurt her, he was her father. She was still reeling over Ryan's departure, so this was really sucky timing. Seriously, could she not catch a break?

"You can come in now," she told him. It's not as though she had a hot date this evening or any plans. "The house is being fixed up a little at a time, so be cautious in the living room. There are probably still some tools out and the trim is lying around."

After brushing past him, Piper unlocked the front door and gestured him inside.

"We can go into the kitchen to get away from this mess." She motioned toward the back of the house. "I can see what I have to eat if you're hungry."

Walker remained in her living area and shook his head. "I didn't come to impose, Piper. But we can talk in the kitchen."

Piper set her purse on the island and went to grab a bottle of water from the fridge. She needed to do something with her hands or he'd see they were not quite so steady. Déjà vu from the experience she'd had in Ryan's kitchen a few days ago.

"Want one?" she asked, holding the cold bottle up.

"No, thanks."

She untwisted the cap and took a drink. What she needed was a beer, but she'd save that for when her father left. She was off work tomorrow and she had every intention of getting good and drunk tonight. She may even sit and watch Lifetime movies just to torture herself further with one happy ending after another.

"I'm sorry this visit is a bit…strained," he told her, taking a seat at her small kitchenette. "I know you're wondering why I just showed up at your house unannounced after all this time."

Piper didn't say a thing as she waited on him to struggle with his own words. In the years she'd lived with him, she'd never seen her father be anything but strong and confident. Now he seemed not only worn and tired, but nervous and unsure.

"What I did, the way I went about handling the divorce and being a father to you, was wrong."

Piper clutched her bottle until the plastic cracked. "If this is—"

"No, Piper." He held up a hand, shaking his head. After tossing his hat onto her table, he continued, "This is something that's been years coming. It needs to be said and you need to hear it."

Nodding, she pursed her lips together. Apparently, Walker Kindred had some sort of guilt laying heavy on him, as well he should. And he was right—this apology was a long time coming.

"I was so caught up in being in the limelight, of being popular and at the top of my game, bringing in more money than we would ever need, I completely lost focus of what was important."

Piper glanced away. God, she was a coward. For years she would've given anything to hear her father say he was sorry, to confess that he was wrong. But now as an adult, she didn't care so much. There was a little girl deep inside her that would forever be scarred by not having her father around, yet seeing him on television smiling and waving to thousands of fans.

She hated being cynical and hard where he was concerned, but she honestly didn't know how to handle this unscheduled, uncomfortable reunion.

"So why are you here now?" she asked, bringing her gaze back to his.

"I have cancer."

Piper was so glad she was leaning against the counter, otherwise she would've fallen to the floor. She set her bottle behind her and wrapped her arms around her waist. Questions whirled around in her head.

She'd been wrong. The hurt could slice deeper. He may have neglected her, may have lived by his own selfish ways, but this was still her father and the word *cancer* brought on a whole host of emotions…namely fear.

She swallowed and held his gaze. "Tell me this isn't a deathbed confession."

Walker shook his head. "Not at all. Actually, I just finished my last chemo treatment and my doctors are confident I'll be perfectly fine."

A wave of relief swept through her. "Good. So you're here because you…"

He came to his feet and crossed the room to stand in front of her. "I'm here because when I was told I had cancer, I immediately thought of what I'd done with my life. The championships I'd won, the people I'd met, the bonds I formed on the road with crew and partners. But there was a huge void in the decades that played out in my head. You and your mother."

Piper cursed the tears that pricked her eyes. Damn vulnerability. Why couldn't she hold it together lately?

"I wanted to wait until I was finished with all of my treatments before I came to see you, to beg you for another chance. I know I missed important years, years I'll never get back, but all I can do is try to be a father now."

Piper sighed. That young girl who lived inside her, the one who'd grown up with a single mother, wanted to throw her arms around the man, take him at his word that he wanted to be part of her life, and forget all that had happened in the past.

But she was not only older now, she was more skeptical.

"It's not that easy. I want it to be—you don't know how much I do," she told him. "But that hurt, that pain that settled in when you left for good, it won't just go away because you were sick and saw the proverbial light."

God, she sounded harsh. She truly didn't mean to be, but how many times could she let her heart lay on the line only to have someone toss it aside for their own self-centered needs.

"I'm not asking for a miracle," he explained, his dark eyes searching hers. "I'll do what you need, go as slow as you like, to see if we can repair or even start fresh with a father-daughter relationship."

"Are you staying in Royal?"

"I'm staying at the small hotel just outside of town," he told her, sliding his hands into his jeans' pockets. "I checked in before I came here."

Piper was torn in so many directions, but she knew there was no way she could in good conscience let her father stay at a hotel. He'd extended the olive branch and now she had to decide whether or not to grab hold.

"We won't be able to get to know each other if you're at a hotel," she said, offering a small smile. "I have a spare room and it's even been freshly painted."

Piper couldn't believe big-time rodeo hotshot Walker

Kindred's eyes misted as a smile spread across his face. Hope speared through her at the thought that this might just work. Her father might finally be ready to be part of her life. Time would tell.

As it would with Ryan.

She sighed. One man at a time.

"I'd really like that," her father told her. "But I don't want you uncomfortable."

Piper shrugged. "I'm not uncomfortable."

"Did I ruin any plans for the night?"

She laughed. "Yeah, I was going to get drunk. Care to join me?"

"I'd love to, but I can't with the meds I'm taking." He smiled. "But I'd be happy to keep popping your tabs for you and work on a beer-amid out of your cans."

Piper laughed as hope spread through her. Maybe they could reconnect and maybe he'd stick through the holidays. Having her father for Thanksgiving would be an awesome gift.

A loud crash sounded through the house. Piper sprang out of bed, her bare feet slapping against the hardwood as she moved into the darkened hallway.

"Dad?" she called.

"I'm fine," he yelled back. "Sorry I woke you."

She followed his voice and found him coming to his feet in the living room. She flicked on the dimmer switch and left it turned down low so the glare from the bulb wouldn't blind them.

"What happened?" she asked.

He laughed, shaking his head. "I was trying to get to the kitchen for some water to take a nausea pill and I tripped over the sawhorse."

"God, I'm so sorry." She glanced at his plaid pajama

bottoms and navy T-shirt. Nothing appeared torn. "Did you hurt yourself?"

"I'm fine," he assured her, placing his hand on the wall for support. "I've taken harder hits falling off angry bulls."

Piper smiled. "Why don't you have a seat and I'll get that glass of water. Do you have your pill?"

He held up a large white pill. "I didn't lose it in the fall."

Laughing, Piper went to get a bottle of water from the fridge. She knew her father was weak from his treatments. She still couldn't get used to seeing him like this, almost frail and, well, older. The once-black hair was now silver and thin from the chemo, the wrinkles around his eyes deeper. The man had lived an entire life without her and now he was here to make amends.

One part of her was thrilled to have her dad back; another part was still skeptical he truly wanted a relationship with her. She couldn't hold back the excitement of getting to know her father again. If he decided to leave, she would be utterly crushed...again.

She honestly believed Walker was here because he loved her and wanted to work at a relationship.

Piper took the water back into the living room and grabbed a seat beside him on the couch.

"Here you go."

After taking his pill, he took another drink and screwed the cap back on. "Sorry again for waking you."

Piper waved a hand. "No problem. I haven't been sleeping that well anyway."

"Problems?"

She eyed him, wanting to laugh for the natural way he asked, but wanting to cry because he genuinely seemed to care and she'd always wanted that father-daughter bond.

"Sorry," he told her with a slight laugh. "I really have no room to ask."

"It's okay." On a sigh, Piper fell back against the cushions. "I'm having an…issue. Nothing I can't handle."

Insomnia, loss of appetite and random bursts of crying, then screaming into an empty room. Yeah, she was handling this breakup quite well. Like a champ.

"I know I have no right to pry," Walker said as he shifted to look at her. "But I'm more than happy to listen, and it's the middle of the night. Since you're not sleeping, we've got nothing else to do."

Piper looked at her father. Another sense of déjà vu settled in. Weeks ago she'd opened up to Ryan in the middle of the night. There was something about darkness that made it easier to open up, easier to not face reality and pretend that there was this special connection.

"I made a stupid mistake and fell in love."

Walker nodded as if he understood.

"And then I made an even stupider mistake and broke it off."

He lifted his brows. "Why was that?"

Piper glanced away, hating how shallow this was going to sound. "I couldn't handle his career decision."

"And what's his career?"

Bringing her eyes back up to his, she said, "Rodeo."

Walker Kindred ran a hand down his face and sighed. He shook his head and let out a laugh.

"God, Piper Jane. I just… I can't even think of what to say." He met her gaze and now hurt stared back at her. "I had no idea my actions would ruin your life."

"Why did you leave?" she asked, emotions clogging her throat. "Why did I never hear from you other than birthdays and Christmas?"

"I let my selfish ways lead my life." He eased back against the cushions, sliding one arm along the back of the sofa. "I wish I could tell you something more tragic, but I was not ready for parenting, or at least not ready for staying home every day, day in and day out. I begged your mother to take you on the road with me. I begged her to homeschool you, but that was selfish of me. Even if you two had joined me, I wouldn't have devoted the time and attention both of you needed."

Piper brushed her hair behind her ear. "I hate your answer, but I appreciate your honesty."

She toyed with the hem of her sleep shorts and wished she could've had her father around to talk to years ago. Even though she wasn't happy with what he told her, she knew he was speaking from his heart and he'd come to her for a fresh start. And honesty was the place to begin if they wanted a firm foundation for building any relationship.

"Who's the cowboy?"

Piper sighed. "Ryan Grant."

Walker's smile widened. "No kidding? Your childhood friend? That man tore up the circuit. It was a shame when he announced his retirement. Wasn't he opening a school or something?"

"A rodeo school for kids," she told him. "He already has most everything ready and had even asked one high school boy to come on full-time in the summer."

"Will he be home for Thanksgiving?"

Piper shrugged. "Honestly, we didn't discuss that."

"You're wishing you hadn't called it quits?"

Shaking her head, Piper groaned. "I don't even know what I wish. I really don't. I wish he hadn't made me fall in love. I wish he hadn't been so damn giving… I wish he hadn't left without even considering me… And I hate that I'm so selfish about it, but I wanted that love. I wanted him and the life he'd laid out for us."

Walker reached out to her cheek to wipe away a tear that Piper hadn't even realized had escaped.

"No man is worth your tears," he whispered. "Including me."

Piper wiped her eyes, hating the vulnerability she had no control over lately. "You're both worth my tears."

Walker started forward as if to hug her, but stopped.

Piper didn't ask, didn't care if she seemed vulnerable. It had been way too long since she'd felt the strong embrace of her father. She reached out, wrapped her arms around his broad shoulders and squeezed.

"Oh, Piper," he murmured as his arms enveloped her. "I've missed you."

Piper cried. Damn it, she couldn't be strong another second. She cried for the little girl who'd never really known her father. She cried for the woman who broke it off with Ryan. And she cried for the reunion she was having because, God help her, she wanted this to last. She wanted this relationship more than she thought possible.

"I love you, Piper," her father whispered.

Piper squeezed her eyes as tears slid down her cheeks. "I love you, too, Dad."

Sixteen

Only one night after the first show, Ryan was already restless. This was not the life he'd wanted, not the life he'd planned when he'd hung up his rope and chosen not to be a Header anymore.

Now he was in a hotel room, same hotel smell and same tacky decor as all the other countless ones over the years. But it had never bothered him before. When he'd sat in his rooms in the past, he'd either have a few beers with his partner or some other members of the circuit or they'd hit a honky-tonk and dance with some mighty fine ladies.

But there was only one lady tonight who he was thinking of. Only one lady who was occupying his time, his thoughts, his every breath. And being on the road was pure hell.

Nearly every second since he'd left, Ryan had wondered what Piper was doing, how she was feeling and if she would ever forgive him. Would she blow him off? Would she try to be all prideful and pretend he hadn't hurt her? Or would she light into him and let him know exactly how much she hated him?

Only seven more weeks until he would officially be done. He would be taking a break for the holidays but he doubted he'd be welcome in her home.

Pain sliced deep through him. Why hadn't he insisted

she come? Why hadn't he done something to make her see he wasn't brushing her or their relationship aside?

Instead of fighting, he'd watched her cry, watched her pour her heart out through tears and then turn and quietly walk out of his life.

What the hell kind of man did that?

A man who didn't think he'd truly lose the woman of his dreams. A small sliver of hope still lived within him that all was not lost, but he hadn't heard a word from her since he'd left. His cell was quiet and Ryan feared with each passing moment of silence, the wedge between them was growing wider and wider. Over the past several days Ryan had pulled out his phone to call her, but he always backed out because he was a coward. The thought of her rejecting him terrified him, so he thought it best to just let her think, let her have some space.

At last night's show, he'd not performed to the best of his abilities because his mind had been elsewhere. Joe would've been better off with another partner who was invested and had his head in the competition. Ryan had merely been filling a spot and nothing more.

Another first for him. Never in all his time on the circuit had he allowed a woman to come between him and the love of his job. No one had ever been important enough or worth the distraction. Distractions could get cowboys hurt; he'd seen it numerous times over the years and had sworn that would never be him.

Because he had to finish what he was doing, help secure Joe that championship cash so he could save his ranch because the man was too prideful to take a handout. But Ryan was going to try again because this scenario of trying to help was not working. Then when Ryan went home, he'd do so with a ring and a promise. He wouldn't leave Piper again.

Ryan was a firm believer that if something was supposed to happen, it would. And in his heart, he knew that he and Piper were not over. They'd hit a bump, one he'd placed in their path, but they would get over it together. If he had to carry her over it, they would make it.

He crossed to the wide window overlooking downtown Dallas and raked a hand through his hair. He should just call her. The worst she could do is tell him to go to hell and hang up, but he really didn't think she would.

He'd been the one to make this mess; the least he could do was try to smooth things over so it didn't get any worse.

Just as he pulled his cell from his jeans' pocket, someone knocked on his door. Confident it wasn't a buckle bunny, since he'd checked in under an alias, he moved through the room and checked the peep hole. His partner, Joe, stood on the other side.

Ryan slid the chain across and opened the door. "What's up?"

"There's a nice group of very interested ladies in the bar downstairs. We were all wondering where you were. Since I'm married, they aren't so interested in me."

It wasn't long ago that he would've been right down there with all of them. And even though the media played him out to be a total player, he truly wasn't. Other than one time he'd had a one-night stand, he'd never taken any wanna-be-cowboy-lovers back to his room.

And there wasn't a woman down there who could even compare to the one woman he was needing tonight. No woman would ever compare to Piper.

"I'm good," he told Joe. "I may turn in early, but I'll see you first thing in the morning."

Joe shook his head and laughed. "Dude, you've got it bad. Why the hell did you agree to come back? You're miserable."

"I wouldn't say miserable," Ryan countered defensively, resting his hand above his head on the door. "I screwed up today, but I'll be back in it tomorrow."

"Ryan, we were partners a long time. I know you." Joe settled his hands on his hips, staring directly into Ryan's eyes. "You don't have off days. You never have. Today was mediocre for some, but for you? I didn't know you could get sidetracked and you did. That right there tells me you don't belong here. Your heart has found somewhere else to be."

Ryan stared at Joe for a second, then busted into a fit of laughter. "Partner, are you watching too many talk shows and getting in touch with your feelings?"

Joe shrugged. "Maybe I don't want to see you throw something away just to win a championship."

"I don't care about winning," Ryan told his partner. "I care about getting that for you."

"When I called you, you never mentioned how fast or how deep your roots were already. I honestly assumed you'd be chomping at the bit to have another round on the circuit, even if there's only seven weeks left in the season."

Ryan nodded. "Probably had you called when I first left, I would've felt that way, but something changed when I went home. I know I went with every intention of starting a school for kids, but there was so much more than that."

He'd fallen in love.

Yeah, he could freely admit it now. He was spurs over chaps in love with Piper Kindred.

"Do I need to search for another partner?" Joe asked, a knowing grin spreading across his face.

Ryan nodded. "It might be best. I won't leave you until you have someone."

Joe nodded. "I'm going to miss you, man. But I've never seen you so unhappy doing something you love. Whoever this woman is, you must love her a whole lot to replace the rodeo."

Ryan laughed. "You remember the rodeo star from when we were younger, Walker Kindred? I'm in love with his daughter."

Joe's eyes widened. "Wow. Wasn't she your best friend in school or something?"

"Yeah. Now she's the woman I'm going to marry."

Joe smiled. "Good for you. We'll start looking for a new partner as soon as possible. If you have to fake an illness or injury to get out, I got your back, partner. Why don't you go on home? We have the next two days off and I'm sure I can ask Dillon to step up."

"Thanks, man." Ryan reached one arm out, pulling his friend into the male version of a hug, one arm around the neck with a hard pat on the back. "Now go tell the ladies I'm taken, as well. Introduce them to Dillon."

Joe lifted his brows. "I'm pretty sure he already went off with a lady earlier. But I'll break the news gently that you're off the market."

After Ryan closed the door, he was more anxious than ever to call Piper. But what if she shot him down? A phone call was so…impersonal. He didn't want to be a coward about this, but he also didn't want to take the easy route, either.

He was only in Dallas. Thankfully they weren't that far from Royal. He'd rent a car and drive. It was only six hours. Or he could check on flights. Surely there was something that would get him home soon. Even if he had to pay a private pilot—that would be the best money he'd ever spent.

But before he could approach her, he had to lay some groundwork. He wanted to be able to go to her with absolute certainty that what they had was real, was the beginning of a lifelong commitment.

* * *

Piper had never made Thanksgiving dinner. Having a dinner for one was so…depressing and a waste of time. But now that her father was back, she figured she'd better at least give it a try. If she botched it up, at least they could laugh and have a good story to tell later.

Walker had gone out to visit some old friends and Piper was juggling groceries while trying to get her key in the back door. Before she could turn the knob, the door flew open and Piper gasped.

"Ryan."

He reached out, taking most of her load from her hands. "I nearly gave up waiting on you to come home," he said, setting the bags on the counter. "How much food do you need here, Red?"

Piper stood in the doorway, still clutching her keys, staring at the one man she didn't think she'd see for at least two more months. Her heart pounded from the initial shock of someone in her house when she thought she'd be alone, but even more than shock was hope. Ryan was back for a reason and she hoped it wasn't just for a turkey dinner.

"What are you doing here?" she asked, totally ignoring his question.

He glanced in the bags and then turned to her, resting a hand on the counter. "Hoping to get you to cook for me."

Piper stepped inside, slowly, still shocked that Ryan was standing in her kitchen. Maybe he'd come back because he'd been injured.

"Are you hurt?" she asked.

"Actually, I am."

Her eyes raked over him, taking in his dark gray shirt and faded jeans, scuffed boots. "You look…" Hot as hell. "Fine."

Stepping closer, Ryan stood toe to toe with her and

grinned. "My heart is broken, Red. You took it when you walked out on me."

That very second tears burned her eyes. "I may have physically walked out, but you left us before I could leave you."

Ryan nodded. "That's a fair statement and one I'm sure you won't let me live down anytime soon. But I've come to the conclusion that I'll put up with you mocking me, so long as you let me back in your life."

"I want to make you suffer," she told him.

He reached for her, cupping her face between his strong hands. "I've suffered, Red. Believe me, I've suffered."

"What about the circuit? Are you just here for Thanksgiving?"

With the holiday being tomorrow, Piper didn't want to jump to conclusions, but neither did she want to give up hope.

Stroking her cheeks with his thumbs, Ryan shook his head. "I'm here for the duration if you'll have me."

A tear slipped over and she blinked the others back. "What about Joe and the championship?"

"I'll think of something," he told her. "If I have to pay off his debt, I'll find a way."

Piper closed her eyes. "Why now, Ryan? Why did you come back?"

"Because watching you walk away was one of the hardest things I've lived through. Because I was miserable without you and because you've gotten into my system. I was a mess out there because you were on my damn mind all the time. You were wreaking havoc on my work."

"So sorry," she said as she met his gaze and offered a half smile.

"You're not sorry, you're gloating." He held her gaze and opened his mouth a couple times before he finally spoke, as if he needed to gather the right words. "I can't be without you again, Piper."

Moisture filled his eyes. In all of their years as friends, she'd only seen him cry at the death of his parents.

"What will happen when you want to leave again? When you get the urge to have an adventure or if someone needs you?"

"First of all, being with you is adventure enough," he informed her.

A laugh escaped her.

"Second—" he nipped at her lips "—the only person that needs me is you."

Piper opened her mouth, ready to defend herself, but he laid a fingertip over her lips.

"And I need you," he murmured. "More than I ever thought possible."

Ryan rested his forehead against hers and sighed. "I'll resort to begging if I need to, Red. But for the love of God, tell me something. Tell me you forgive me or you'll think about it. Anything."

Piper smiled. "As much as I'd love to see you groveling, I'll cut you some slack."

"Does that mean you love me?"

She wrapped her arms around his waist and held on, not ready to let go anytime soon. "It means if you try to leave again, I'll castrate you."

Ryan picked her up, spun her around and kissed her. Hands-in-her-hair, devouring-her-lips, making-her-breathless-with-want kissed her. Yeah, they would have one hell of a reunion tonight.

"Uh, should I come back later?"

Piper jumped back. She'd been so caught up in the blissful moment she hadn't heard the back door open, nor had she heard her father step in. While she wasn't a teen, she was still embarrassed that he'd seen her getting hot and heavy with Ryan.

"Piper?" Ryan asked, glancing between her father and her.

She smiled. "A lot happened while you were gone."

Walker stepped forward, extending his hand. "From what I heard and saw, I think I should say welcome to the family."

Piper and Ryan laughed.

"He hasn't proposed, Dad."

Ryan shook Walker's hand. "No, I haven't. I think he just did it for me."

Stepping back and sliding his hand into his pocket, he pulled out a small box. Lifting the lid, he got down on one knee.

"I know you aren't one for mushy or traditional things," he started, "but I have to propose the right way."

Piper stared at the simple band of diamonds. Placing a hand over her mouth, she tried not to start crying again like some lovesick woman.

"I've loved you since you punched me in my face. I've never met anyone who cares for people the way you do. I'm not worthy of your love, but I'm asking for it anyway."

From the corner of her eye, Piper saw her father step back. The fact that he was present for the most important moment of her life was not lost on her. He had been absent for nearly everything, but now, when she was starting a new chapter, he was there.

"The band is flat because you work with your hands a lot, but we can get something else if you want."

Piper grabbed his hands and tugged until he came back to his feet to stand in front of her. "This is perfect," she told him.

"It's got diamonds all the way around and it's called a

Forever band." He removed the ring and slid it onto her finger. "I didn't want traditional, not for you. And forever seemed to sum up my feelings perfectly."

Piper stared down at the band on her finger and couldn't suppress her tears or her smile. She'd cried so much lately, but she didn't care. Ryan had come back to her and so had her father. All those tears were worth it.

"You were pretty sure of yourself, cowboy." She looked back up at him. "Coming here with a ring."

"I wasn't sure of myself. I was a nervous wreck. But I was sure of us."

Piper threw her arms around Ryan and whispered in his ear, "I love you. And when my father isn't looking, I'll show you just how much."

He wrapped his arms around her and whispered back, "Can you send him to the store for more groceries?"

"Okay," Walker said across the room. "I may be old, but I can still hear. You two need privacy. I'll just go…out. Somewhere. For a few hours. Um…yeah, I'll find somewhere."

Piper laughed at her father's stuttering, his red face. "Seriously, Dad. You can stay. I love having the two most important men in my life here with me. Besides, I have no clue how to get started on preparing this Thanksgiving feast for tomorrow."

Ryan stepped back, unbuttoned his cuffs and rolled up his sleeves. "Well, Red, you're in luck. I used to help my mama in the kitchen and Thanksgiving was her specialty."

As they started preparing dressing and pies, Piper's heart swelled. In her tiny, remodeled kitchen they worked and she couldn't have been happier. Ryan and her father spoke of the rodeo. They'd traveled on two separate circuits, but the level of respect was evident from both men.

"And you needed to help your partner?" Walker asked.

"Did he find someone to fill in already? Someone as good as you?"

Ryan shrugged as he continued to tear bread and throw it in the bowl for the stuffing. "He's no slacker. I just worry about Joe not getting that championship money."

"I'll give it to him," Walker said easily.

Piper spun around from the counter where she'd been pouring filling into a pie crust. "What?"

"I told you I worked my ass off and have more money than I know what to do with."

Piper's gaze shot to Ryan's, then back to her dad's. "Wow, um. That's great, Dad."

Ryan nodded. "If you're serious, Walker, then we'll split it, but it's not necessary for you to pitch in. I had already thought of just giving Joe the money so he could relax and not be so stressed and his family wouldn't have to worry anymore."

"Fine then." Walker smiled. "Damn, I'm glad I'm back home."

Piper knew in her heart Ryan was here to stay. The man hadn't been gone too long before he realized where his heart belonged and she was quite certain that had a friend not needed him to begin with, he never would've left.

Piper crossed the room and bent to hug her father. "I'm glad you're back, too. This will be the most memorable Thanksgiving ever."

Seventeen

Ryan closed and locked the bedroom door. He didn't know what had shocked him more today, that Piper had agreed to marry him or that her father was back and they seemed to be building a relationship. He'd give anything to have his parents back and he was proud of Piper for giving her father another chance.

She came out of the bathroom wearing a short, silky black gown that stopped at midthigh and had a deep vee in the front.

"God, I've missed your lingerie," he said.

Piper laughed. "As opposed to my sunny disposition and my snarky comments?"

"I've missed it all." He pushed off the door and started unbuttoning his shirt. "I never want to be away from you again."

Piper held his gaze. "On that we can agree. I was miserable and then when Dad came I was even more torn up. But you're both here, you're both in my life and I can't ask for more."

"I'm surprised you seem so comfortable with your dad. Did you two have a fast reunion?"

She nodded, holding on to the post of the bed. "He has cancer."

"My God, Piper." Ryan froze. "Is he okay? Are you?"

"I'm okay and so is he. He's finished his treatments and the doctors say he's well on his way to recovery. But he told me it made him realize what was important. At first I was angry that it took a potentially terminal illness to wake him up, but then I decided I had a second chance and if he was willing to try, then so was I."

Ryan shrugged out of his shirt, tossed it aside and made fast work of his boots, socks and jeans. Standing in only his boxer briefs, he crossed to her.

"I'm glad you've been in the mood for second chances lately."

She tipped her face up to meet his and smiled. "I'm not as hard as I used to be. I guess that's what love does to you."

He slid his hands around her waist and tugged her against him. "Say it again. I'll never tire of hearing you say you love me."

She looped her arms around his neck. "I do, Ryan. I love you so much that I was completely shattered when you left."

Ryan didn't want to focus on the negative and he sure as hell didn't want to think about the ass he'd been.

"Let's look forward," he told her, nipping her lips. "Let's pretend I wasn't a jerk and now that my priorities are in the right order, we can start planning our wedding. Because I can't wait until you are Mrs. Piper Grant."

A wide smile spread across her freshly washed face. "I love how that sounds."

His hands slid up her bare arms. Taking her thin straps, he eased them down. "I love how you dress for me," he whispered. "I love how I can peel you out of this in no time. And I love how you feel around me."

The straps rested on her biceps and she slipped her arms free. The material hung on her breasts until Ryan gave one swift tug and sent the garment to the floor with a whoosh. She stepped out of it and stood in front of him wearing nothing but his ring.

"You undo me, Piper." His eyes raked over her as he ridded himself of his briefs. "I'm nothing without you."

"Show me," she told him as she held out her hands and led him toward the bed.

He tumbled down on top of her, sinking into the plush comforter. Easing her legs apart, he settled between her hips.

Resting his elbows beside her head, he lifted his body slightly. Watching her face, her parted lips, her soft eyes, Ryan slid into her in a slow, deliberate move that had her arching her back and closing her eyes.

"Look at me," he whispered. "Always look at me, at us."

Her eyes locked on to his and he felt her love, her power, all the way to his heart.

Her ankles locked behind his back as her hips lifted beneath his. Ryan knew she wanted fast and rough, but he wanted slow and memorable.

Setting the pace he wanted, he leaned down, kissed her lips then slid his mouth down the column of her throat until he found one pert nipple. When he clamped his mouth around her, she tightened her grip with her knees on his sides.

Her hips pumped faster and Ryan lifted his head. "You're in such a hurry."

"And you're not moving fast enough," she told him.

Ryan smiled, turning his attention to the other breast as he eased in and out of her. But there was only so much control he had and, when she tightened around him, he knew she was close.

Reaching down, he slid a hand between them and touched

her in her most intimate area. In no time Piper stilled, her body tensed as she bowed and cried out his name.

There was no more beautiful sight than Piper beneath him, coming undone, with his name on her lips. And because he'd held back as long as he could, Ryan gave one last thrust and allowed his climax to overtake him, reveling in the fact this was just the beginning of the best days of his life.

When their tremors ceased, Ryan eased down on top of her, stroking her side and whispering, "I love you" in her ear because he never wanted her to doubt it again.

"Are we going to have a big wedding?" he asked, rolling over just enough so he wasn't squashing her. "I imagine all of our friends will want to come since they've invited us to theirs."

Piper laced her fingers with his and rested their joined hands on her flat stomach. "I never wanted a big wedding, but I suppose we need to invite all of our friends."

"Do what you want, Piper," he told her. "If you want to fly to Vegas, we'll fly there tonight. If you want to plan something, we'll plan it."

Ryan watched the play of emotions on her face. Her brows were drawn, but then her eyes widened and a wide smile spread across her face.

"I'm going to need a real wedding," she told him, turning her head to meet his gaze. "Nothing elaborate. We can marry at your ranch. I'd like it outside with our closest friends."

Ryan grinned. "Sounds good to me."

"And I want my father to walk me down the aisle."

Ryan searched her face and nodded. "He would love that."

Piper sighed, snuggling deeper against him. "Timing is everything and I believe he came back now for a reason."

Ryan wrapped his arm around her and pulled her close. There was nothing that satisfied him more than seeing Piper so happy, so content.

"I never thought I'd marry you," he whispered. "I always knew I loved you, but I never thought I actually had a chance at winning your heart."

Her face tipped up to his. "Oh, you won my heart, cowboy. Now you're going to have a long, long time with your prize."

Ryan kissed the tip of her nose. "Best prize I ever won."

* * * * *

TEXAS CATTLEMAN'S CLUB:
THE MISSING MOGUL
Don't miss a single story!

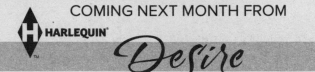
#2263 THE SECRET HEIR OF SUNSET RANCH

The Slades of Sunset Ranch • by Charlene Sands

Rancher Justin Slade returns from war a hero...and finds out he's a father. But as things with his former fling heat back up, he must keep their child's paternity secret—someone's life depends on it.

#2264 TO TAME A COWBOY

Texas Cattleman's Club: The Missing Mogul
by Jules Bennett

When rodeo star Ryan Grant decides to hang up his spurs and settle down, he resolves to wrangle the heart of his childhood friend. But will she let herself be caught by this untamable cowboy?

#2265 CLAIMING HIS OWN

Billionaires and Babies • by Olivia Gates

Russian tycoon Maksim refuses to become like his abusive father, so he leaves the woman he loves and their son. But now he's returned a changed man...ready to stake his claim.

#2266 ONE TEXAS NIGHT...

Lone Star Legacy • by Sara Orwig

After a forbidden night of passion with his best friend's sister, Jared Weston gets a second chance. But can this risk taker convince the cautious Allison to risk it all on him?

#2267 EXPECTING A BOLTON BABY

The Bolton Brothers • by Sarah M. Anderson

One night with his investor's daughter shouldn't have led to more, but when she announces she's pregnant, real estate mogul Bobby Bolton must decide what's more important—family or money.

#2268 THE PREGNANCY PLOT

by Paula Roe

AJ wants a baby, and her ex is the perfect donor. But their simple baby plan turns complicated when Matt decides he wants a second chance with the one who got away!

YOU CAN FIND MORE INFORMATION ON UPCOMING HARLEQUIN® TITLES, FREE EXCERPTS AND MORE AT WWW.HARLEQUIN.COM.

HDCNM1013

SPECIAL EXCERPT FROM

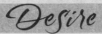

HARLEQUIN®

Desire

USA TODAY *bestselling author*

Janice Maynard

presents

A BILLIONAIRE FOR CHRISTMAS

Available December 2013 from Harlequin Desire!

Phoebe opened her front door with some trepidation. Not because she had anything to fear from the man on the porch. She'd been expecting him for several hours. What she dreaded was telling him the truth.

She backed up, and he entered, sucking all the air out of the room. He was a big man, built like a lumberjack, broad through the shoulders, and tall. His thick, wavy chestnut hair gleamed with health. The glow from the fire that crackled in the hearth picked out strands of dark gold.

When he removed his jacket, she saw that he wore a deep blue sweater along with dark dress pants. The faint whiff of his aftershave mixed with the unmistakable scent of the outdoors. He filled the room with his presence.

Reaching around him gingerly, she flipped on the overhead light, sighing inwardly in relief when the intimacy of firelight gave way to a less cozy atmosphere.

He gave her home a cursory glance, then settled his sharp gaze on her face. His masculine features were put together in a pleasing fashion, but the overall impression was intensely male. Strong nose, noble forehead, chiseled jaw, and lips made for kissing a woman.

His scowl grew deeper. "I'm tired as hell, and I'm starving. If you could point me to my cabin, I'd like to get settled for the night, Ms….?"

"Kemper. Phoebe Kemper. You can call me Phoebe." Oh, wow. His voice, low and gravelly, stroked over her frazzled nerves like a lover's caress. The faint Georgia drawl did nothing to disguise the hint of command. This was a man accustomed to calling the shots.

She swallowed, rubbing damp palms on her thighs. "I have a pot of vegetable beef stew still warm on the stove. You're welcome to have some."

The aura of disgruntlement he wore faded a bit, replaced by a rueful smile. "That sounds wonderful."

She waved a hand. "Bathroom's down the hall. I'll get everything on the table."

"And afterward you'll show me my lodgings?"

Gulp. "Of course."

He was most likely going to be furious with her, no matter how she tried to spin the facts.

Because his lodgings had been destroyed in the storm and the only bed left for miles was in this cabin—with her.

Don't miss

A BILLIONAIRE FOR CHRISTMAS

Available December 2013 from Harlequin Desire!